Eliza Robertson, Kevin Couture & Jill Sexsmith

COMING ATTRACTIONS
12

The publishers acknowledge the support of the Canada Council for the Arts, the Government of Ontario through the Ontario Media Development Corporation and the Government of Canada through the Canada Book Fund for their publishing activities.

"Here Be Dragons" by Eliza Robertson and "Play the Dying Card" by Jill Sexsmith first appeared in *The New Quarterly*; "Bear Cub" and "Lemonade Free" by Kevin Couture and "The Problem with Babies" and "A Box Full of Wildebeest" by Jill Sexsmith were first published in *The Fiddlehead*; "My Sister Sang" by Eliza Robertson originally appeared in *Grain*; "Roadnotes" by Eliza Robertson was originally published in *PRISM international*.

ISBN 978 0 7780 1387 7 (hardcover)
ISBN 978 0 7780 1389 1 (softcover)

Cover art by Cyril Power
Book design by Michael Macklem

Printed in Canada

PUBLISHED IN CANADA BY OBERON PRESS

Canada Council   Conseil des Arts
for the Arts   du Canada

Contents

INTRODUCTION

I am writing this from the Gaspé Peninsula, an astounding place where sleek manic gannets divebomb the sea and feeding whales breathe and dive and breathe and dive. This bay is a place of rich treasures and euphoric variety; I hope you find some of the same riches and variety collected in this season's *Coming Attractions*, fresh new short stories from Eliza Robertson, Kevin Couture and Jill Sexsmith.

A slick young writer, Eliza Robertson was born in Vancouver, and took her undergraduate degree at the University of Victoria. She lives in France now, after completing her Masters of Prose Fiction in England at the University of East Anglia, where she won the Man Booker Scholarship. Her stories have appeared in journals in Canada, the United Kingdom and the United States, and have been shortlisted for National Magazine Awards and the McClelland & Stewart Journey Prize. She is writing a novel and gathering stories for her first collection.

Kevin Couture was raised in a small mining town and now lives in Victoria. His writing has appeared in a number of publications including *Grain, The Fiddlehead, The Antigonish Review, The Dalhousie Review, Event, Prairie Fire* and *PRISM international*, and his insightful stories have a variety of voices and tones, dealing with bear cubs and bear mothers, lemonade stands and the Twelve Steps, accidents and scapegoats. He is the recipient of the 2011 Micro Award for flash fiction.

Jill Sexsmith grew up in Manitoba and has lived and worked in Australia and Japan. Her writing is chameleon and possesses a weird humour, touching down in Asia, Africa, Paris, Moscow and Mumbai, and always home. She is a graduate of the University of British Columbia's Master of Fine Arts optional-residency program, lives in Winnipeg, and works in communications for the University of Manitoba. She has appeared in journals such as *Prism international, The New Quarterly, The Fiddlehead,* and *Walrus.*

MARK ANTHONY JARMAN

Contributions for Coming Attractions 13, *published or unpublished, should be sent to Oberon Press, 205–145 Spruce Street, Ottawa, Ontario K1R 6P1 before 31 March, 2013. All manuscripts should enclose a stamped self-addressed envelope.*

ELIZA ROBERTSON

Here Be Dragons

LISBON

At the café on Rua Garrett, you are the woman who serves me sardines. I pose European under a yolk-gold umbrella. She threads through tables pelvis-first, answers queries on wine: From the Minho region, No the colour is not green, In Portuguese we pronounce it *verde*. Like yours, her eyes are the India ink spills labelled as islands by our forebears. And her hair. Her hair defies Neatlines. Had I known this spot was so hot for tourists, for burnt-cheeked Britons and McAmericans, university gals with backpacks and Birkenstocks, their boyfriends with hacky sacks and pony tails, had I known this I'd have ordered my fish from a hole-in-the-whitewashed-wall of Miradouro de Santa Luzia. But then I'd have missed you. Like you she wears black curls thick enough to catch bees. Faded jeans, high-waist-wide-hips, and a sea green top that clings to the contours of her Northern Hemisphere. But what really grabs me, what really clutches me by the collar and flashes me back is how she hangs behind the bar between orders. Pregnant gulps from an under-the-counter *pintada*, then back at my table, lips wet with foam. The extent of your career as a waitress may be merCator, but you punctuated your work just the same.

To my left, a Tampa Bay fan with a blond mullet pretends to be Canadian: I'm from the capital, you know, Toronto, you know. East of me, a woman from Toronto pretends to be Canadian: So the ferries to Vancouver went on strike, So why didn't you just drive? I want to tell you and Our Lady of the Immaculate Tables that I'm not like them. I'm here on business. To ink lines on paper, call them roads, to graph cities over grids. To define place. Instead I say, Portuguese sardines are bigger than the ones back home. Truly, its spine stretches across my plate like a rat's tail. Our Lady of the Immaculate

Tables looks beyond me and asks if I'll order another *cerveja*.

At Ribeira Market, I buy a pear and a bag of pine nuts, then hop the *Elevador da Bica*. Lisbon, like Rome, is a city built on seven hills. But the Portuguese carved tracks into their cobblestones, fit the tracks with aluminum shoeboxes, wide-windowed and painted sunny, four in total, to chug tourists and locals twenty-a-time up the narrow intra-wall slopes. On the *Elevador da Bica* you are the Portuguese mother of two, breastfeeding one and scolding the second for peeling gum off the seat. This time it's the way she is not ashamed. To breastfeed, to sculpt P's with spit (*P-or favor*), to wear her brows thick and a shadow above the lip. I like that you never used bleach.

Girl of the Seat Gum can't be older than six. Her hair is tied with a dark green scarf, the boiled spinach shade of lower elevations, and her forehead is bridged with a symmetrically pristine unibrow. I offer Girl of the Seat Gum a handful of pine nuts and she looks to her mother, who nods and switches breasts.

You who met your zenith before we had children to peel gum off seats. You who died On Business, K.I.A.: calves plush with rash and a forehead I could sauté garlic on. *Pro bono* land survey for the new primary school in Arusha, and we popped enough Larium to dream technicolour for a month. But there's no fix for Dengue, the Breakbone, no Preventative Measures beyond long sleeves and repellent. You who hated repellent, the smell of science-pickled eyeballs, the way it made your fingers sticky, the way you could taste it in your morning *chapatti*. K.I.A., but That Was Africa. Shit happens, *hakuna matada*. You always as crazy cool as bananas in the refrigerator. You, the centre of my celestial sphere.

The *elevador* inches between walls with washlines that hang skirts and neon bras like prayer flags. It takes two left turns without a rise in elevation before I realize we've peaked. Disembarking at Miradouro de Santa Catarina is like disembarking at Grouse Mountain except this tram runs on tracks, and instead of evergreens there are white box buildings, and instead of you fingering our initials into breath on the window, there's Our Mother of the Ample Bosom forbidding her daughter to throw pine nuts at pigeons. West of a sandwich-and-wine terrace, there's an oval lawn and the Adamastor. Spirit of the Cape, Gatekeeper of the Indian Ocean, heavy jowls and unkempt beard/scowling from shrunken, hollow eyes/…mouth coal black, teeth yellow with decay. I taunt the Adamastor with nuts. I smear sardine fingers into the stony bulges of his nostrils. I say Come And Get Me. Four shirtless men sit on the wall that encloses the lawn, and when I turn from the monster they're staring and one of them hucks a can.

At the Church of Our Lady Queen of Martyrs, you are the nun with gap teeth and two-toned eyes. Heterochromia, she says. One yellow, one brown. Two-Toned carries wood sorrel with both hands like it's a snake and leads me down white brick steps to the courtyard. She tosses the sorrel into the disputed hedge of the neighbouring vineyard and I set up the tripod for my theodolite. Hired by God this round, or at least one of His Portuguese ambassadors, to define the property lines between church and grape—A matter to be settled posthaste, said the abbot over the telephone, They've cut off the free wine.

The machine is two silver panels on either side of a lens, and when I'm feeling congenial I call it my Cyclops. I centre my x on God and grapes' distant wall and align my y with local gravity. I am Lee Harvey Oswald because my eyes blink through crosshairs. Because *triangulate* sounds so violent.

Two-Toned wears a grey veil and no habit. Rosary beads hook from the belt loops of her jeans and as she walks a wooden cross bounces against her hip. You become her when she stands beside a shrub to collect quinces with a priest's black biretta. She sings Nancy Sinatra and plays card tower with the fruit in the hat, the quinces yellow and knobbed like cancerous lemons. These boots are made for walkin', and that's just what they'll do. And then there's you in the valley gathering cherries in the belly of your May The Forks Be With You apron, humming something bluesy that neither of us know the name of.

Two-Toned sees I'm watching her instead of the theodolite and tosses me a quince. You know how to play with *marmelos*, she says, and I answer How. It's a game for the sea, a group game, catch-and-swim. *Marmelos* are sour, but sweet with salt water. So the first person pitches and everyone swims, and whoever fetches the *marmelo* first takes a bite and pitches again, and everyone swims, over and over 'til it's eaten. Catch the Quince, I say, How charming. And to think back home we're stuck spinning bottles. You have *esposa*, she replies, A wife. I say Oh. I say Not yet, but I'm engaged.

After my romp with Pythagoras in the crosshairs I want the Bigger Picture, the three-sixty, so Two-Toned leads me back up the helix of white bricks to the church's roof, to the panoramic view. The wall up here is painted blue on white ceramic tiles. It's a sea mural, bordered by vases and ropes of flowers and pillars that rest on the plump shoulders of cherubs. In the scene, azure women arch from arcs of azure spray, and waves swell over a cliff until my eyes adjust and I realize the waves are the manes of rearing horses.

Two-Toned sits now before a bench stacked with faded tiles and fist-sized jars of paint. I restore *azujelos* she says, and dabs a blue slicked brush into the shadow of what might be a cherub's belly button. Of course you do, I say. My fiancée restored maps.

I step onto the strip of clay tiles that border the roof's edge. I see vineyards and pear trees, plump jade acres that are eventually flattened by the bleached walls of a nearby township. I wager with myself the distance between that steeple and that chimney, and that chimney and me, and me and the ground, and I add up my angles: the angles it takes to join the one-

13

eighty. To leap into the antimeridian, the y-axis. To bisect my horizon.

St. Petersburg

Palace Square at 4:45 in the Ante Meridiem inspires me to reinstate the Tsar. A city of four and a half million people and I stand with my Cyclops in a 40,000-square-metre expanse of silence. The facade parabolas across the square, and I am the focus point to its vertex. The lonely guy in a beaver pelt *ushanka* opposite Triumphal Arch. My assignment: to collect data for a three-dimensional three-sixty online interactive tour map to end all tour maps.

It occurs to me that I'm listening to a series of chinks, and a shoulder-check reveals a heavy-coated security guard in a navy blue saucer cap, leaning against the base of the Alexander Column. He's clipping his fingernails. A grey sliver zings toward me.

A good one, he says, and I don't know if he means the shot or the nail. The blades chime together again and a clipping drops onto his shoe. I say Privet and try to recall if it translates to Hello or Thanks or Toilet. Privet, he says. I tell him I'm here to collect data. You are map man, he says. Da, I reply, I am Map Man. He peers through the wrong side of my Cyploptic lens and says, Eet's hard? I say Easier than it looks and he replies, Da, da, the casket open in simple way. He tells me Inside is warmer, and asks if I like art. So I bag One-Eye, collapse the tripod and follow him into the far left entrance.

In Winter Palace you are Elizabeth Petrovna in *Portrait of Elizabeth Petrovna on Horseback Accompanied by a Negro Servant*. The painting hangs at the end of a gilded hall: velvet carpet, vaulted ceilings, pillars that drip gold leaf and angel hair. You're jaunty in a tricorn hat and riding coat, avocado-green, wide cuffs, white gloves. Tall-piped boots that end above the knee, a length disproportionate to the foot on the stirrup. The mare's tail flows like it's been brushed in the mirror 100 strokes a day, and the Negro Servant is clad like a petit prince: white tights, pink sash, gold-braid blouse. Far cry from the Maasai warrior who led our camel in sandy circles from Museum to Genuine Maasai Village, his toes chalky inside the tire sandals, heels white from dust and callus.

Behind me, the guard says I'm not me, this horse isn't mine, and I am not a cabman. I turn from you to respond with an arched, Come Again? brow, and he says Whether you hit an owl with a stump or the stump with an owl, it's the owl who suffers. I smile diplomatic and ask Where's a good place 'round here to eat.

At Vlad's Vodka House, you are the emaciated barmaid who calls herself a countess. She sits across from me over a beer-ringed tablecloth, linguine legs folded under her chin like a spring. She brought me six rounds of vodka On Zee House and said, I have six more Rounds, Vant To See?

Russians plop O's from their mouths like teaspoons of caviar. O. Go. Go, says the Countess as she thrusts the butt of her .44 calibre into my palm. She clasps my wrist, guides the gun's muzzle up her throat, traces it along her lips, and plays Lifeguard, Mouth-To-Mouth. She says You first. She says Take a spin. Her breath reeks of pickled cabbage. I say No, Nyet. The barrel is long and dainty, the revolver older than Tsar Nicholas II. I say, What a handle! Is it walnut? Six cylinders, she says, One in six, I'm Not Scared, Go.

The pub is empty save the fat man counting cash and smoking cigarettes on a barstool. The Union fell twenty years ago but Vlad has yet to update decor, the walls cluttered with portraits of Uncle Lenin and posters I can't read that shout Who Are You With and Workers Unite and Nowhere But Mosselprom. When the Countess grins, her lips stretch like the Neva River in an upside down map of Petersburg. Coward, she says, My turn then. She flips the revolver in my hand so that the muzzle stares me in the third eye.

You and I had propped the card table five clicks west of Mission Harbour Station. We poured earl grey from the claw-footed pot of your mother's silver service. The tea party an *ad hoc* finale to the binge that followed our final finals of under-grad—rum gulped from globe-glasses sharpied with rhumb lines, the twenty-sixer of Lemon Hart a cherry to top our two-scoop geography degree sundae. The loose leaf had over-steeped from the truck ride, but the tannins tasted familiar and vaguely reassuring. Truth or Dare, you had said after we ran out of rum, But if you choose Truth, you're a sissy. So we perched stiff and English, arrow spines, ankles crossed tidy, and we spoke in the Queen's tongue, in Henry Higgins, all Rain in Spain, How Now Brown Cow—I asked for the sugar If You Please and you replied Of Course, My Squashed Cabbage Leaf. When the tracks trembled with the weight of the a.m. *Canadian* barrelling eastbound from Vancouver, we stared at ourselves in the reflections of one another's eyes, dared to sip tea when our ears buzzed with whistle. I blinked first, charged you and the table from the tracks—though in the end we had a good twenty seconds. Enough time for you to thumb a penny from your pocket and plant it on the rail.

And now my ears buzz with the Euro Pop that leaks tinny from the sound system, the mouth of the Tsarist revolver pinned cold to the bridge of my nose. The backs of my arms prickle when the Countess lights a cigarette and I realize that now the hand on the grip is my own. I close my eyes and see the city projected against my eyelids, a tourism montage: onion domes that blister jewels, cavernous ceilings painted with kings for kings, rearing bridges, rearing horses, all of it drenched in the ghoulish mirage of you.

Ruletka, the Countess says, Spin the cylinder. I push the thumbpiece until the chamber clucks open, roll the cylinder and count holes until I find one clogged with a bullet. Eyes closed, says the Countess, so I shut my lids and rotate the chamber back and forth with my thumb, humming to not track rounds. My palm folds the chamber back with a *click*

and with a *click* I tap the hammer and squeeze the trigger
and: *click*.

ARUSHA

At the centre of Africa between Cairo and Cape Town, a dove-
haired woman sniffs mangoes from a wooden wheelbarrow.
The vendor peels oranges with a machete and speaks to a
woman shucking corn on the pavement beside her bowl of
embers. Follows Her Nose wears high-waisted khakis and a
white sleeveless blouse, and she looks like someone 60 who
passes for 45, her cheeks slack without droop. I watch from
my tin chair at the Patisserie to see if she checks avocados like
you, light squeeze in the palm of your hand. She does not.
    Mount Meru looms over the city as crisp and conical as a
bent elbow. A Maasai elder saunters up Sokoine with a gait
steady enough to continue him North over the slope. Land
Rovers and *dala-dalas* maelstrom 'round the roundabout—a
herd of metal elephants, Carousel Africa on Stampede Speed.
The murals on *dala-dala* windshields read like an atlas index:
Hollywood, Jerusalem. Da Bronx. The elder is unphased by
the whirl of steel, our world of steel. As he threads through
vehicles his ear lobes swing like balance balls. A rover barrels
behind him and I lose sight until he arrives whole on the
other side. He hoods his blanket over his head and ambles
away under a canopy of sidewalk trees.
    At the primary school in Mianzini I sit opposite the head-
mistress with clouds in her hair. She lounges pensive in a donated recliner, seventies velvet stretched over cushion like
grafted skin. Her girl aerosols the cloud from an aluminum
can, massages puffs into the black nest of her weave. She looks
queenly in a burgundy pantsuit, luminous and rotund,
buxom cheeks and eyes that chirp. Sit, she says, Take bites
and chai. After a flutter of Swahili a second girl sails into the
office with a blue thermos and donuts, umbrella patterned

17

kitangi knotted around her waist. She stirs my tea and plugs the wet spoon back into the sugar bowl. Outside the screen door, a wire-haired baby rolls in the gravel with a newborn pup. Her giggles rise into the banana leaves like bubbles inside a glass bottle of Fanta. Last time, you sat beside me, and I remember you drank Fanta instead of chai because you thought the carbonation might Do Your Stomach Good, like ginger-ale, because you felt a Touch Queasy, and I remember that the Fanta haloed your lips orange. Headmistress says *Pole, Pole sana*, which means she is Sorry, very sorry for my loss or her country's mosquitoes, or your distaste for repellant, the way it made your palms so sticky-like-skin-under-Band-Aids, or for my cod liver cheeks, the grey bags beneath my eyes.

In the room we rented on Fire Road, I dragged our bed onto the balcony because your muscle joints could brand cows, because inside was Too, too, too, too..., because the oxygen between walls clogged your throat. Seven p.m. and the sun en route to the other side of the world, sub-equator sky as unfamiliar as a friend after a car crash, stars scrambled like dice. Yahtzee. The stone pillars of the front gate were spiked with broken bottle glass, amber and green triangles that glinted with the occasional sweep of the guard's flashlight. Your head in my lap, hair like an oil spill, wet black knots splayed across my thigh. I cheered you with puns. Your cheeks hot, eyelids a-flutter. A map is like a fish because They both have scales. You don't have to understand everything about geographic information systems, as long as you get the GIS of it. How do geographers find the girl they're going to marry? They datum.

I fingered through your knots, memorized the curls, calculated the angles between cowlicks. Your hair streamed in kinks, black rivers that wound east and west and north from your skull, two centimetres above scalp-level. Lush plains, low elevations, save the downy helixes that corkscrewed from the coast of your ear. I wanted to preserve you, to shade you

18

from direct sunlight, store you in optimal humidity within an acid-free frame. I wanted to make you a Legend.

My Sister Sang

Seated and stowed.
    Thank you, all set.
    [Sound like cockpit door closing.]
    Oh, that fucking door again.
    What's wrong?
    This.
    Oh.
    You have to slam it pretty hard.
    [Sound like cockpit door closing.]

———

This one is: Plane Ditched in Columbia River After Multiple Bird Strikes. Three serious injuries. One fatality. Forty-three passengers treated for hypothermia. On my desk Monday morning: the stats, the snaps, the autopsy, the tapes. (The .FLAC files.) (We still say tapes.) Linguists identify speech— loss of thrust, loss of trust, one five zero knots, one five zero, not. I take the acoustics. Engine noise, aircraft chimes, whether the captain has reclined his seat.

———

Flaps one, please.
    Flaps one.
    What a view of the Columbia today.
    Yeah.
    After takeoff checklist.
    After takeoff checklist complete.
    [Sound of chime.]
    Birds.
    Whoa.
    [Sound of thump.]

Oh shit.
Oh yeah.
Uh oh.

———

Sometimes you hear the pilots snap photos. Would you look at those Rockies, or photo of the FO clicking a photo of that fighter. Also, they swap jokes.
Welcome to the George Herbert Walker Bush Intergalactical Airport.
[Sound of laugh.]
I can't fly anymore. Free flights, if I wanted, but I can't coax myself past security. I take trains.

———

Mayday mayday mayday mayday.
Caution, terrain terrain terrain.
Too low. Terrain.
Pull up. Terrain.
We're goin' in the river.
Say again, Jetblue?
Pull up. Pull up. Pull up. Pull up. Pull up.

———

The *Oregonian* featured the accident front page. I bought a copy at lunch. The girl's on A3: Backup Singer Dies In Plane Crash. In the photo, she's surrounded by honeycomb. Her hair's the same colour. Yellow in the waxlight, how sun warms through a sheet of gold tack.

———

Name: VERNON, Joy. Case #1734512, age 19, race white,

sex female.

    Cause of death: cerebral hypoxia
          due to: asphyxiation
          due to: aspiration of water into the air passages
    Manner of death: drowning

In the autopsy photo, her eyes are open. Brown irises. Eyes like wood like warm like walnut. Report says sclerae clear. Report says ears pierced once each lobe and nose unremarkable.

She sang back-up for Fiona Apple, says the newspaper. And LuAnne de Lesseps. She also released a single of her own, which you can purchase on iTunes for $1.29.

My sister sang before she married. Christian pop, which her manager sold as gospel. We weren't religious. Our car had a Darwin fish. But her manager said there was a market. He said, *Praise radio will eat her up with double catsup and a side of fries.*

    I never liked him. He wore T-shirts with milk stained down the front. Cheerios, he'd say. Sometimes it's so hard to get them in the mouth.

The new linguist started today. She'll analyze the resonant frequencies of vocal tracts. F-values, she calls them. How we form words from the lips and the teeth and the tongue and the lungs. She combs her hair very smooth. I think she must use a bun-setter.

I brought a coffee to her computer station to introduce myself. I said, "Well if it doesn't work out here, I think the CIA is hiring."

She typed the rest of her sentence, then pointed to the small ceramic pig on her desk. It wore a post-it. The post-it said, *Cunning linguist jokes: $1.*

She's bright. But she knows she's bright, which makes it less attractive. Still.

————

We work in the basement where you don't see the sun. You see: two computer monitors with equalizer waves; desks made from highly recyclable aluminum; ergonomic chairs, whirly. Our lab is fragrance-free and climate-controlled, volume-controlled, light-controlled. Plants cannot grow here. We keep a synthetic lemon tree by the vending machine.

————

To isolate the voices on a CVR tape, you have to clear the extraneous noise in layers. The engine roar, the static. Like filing sand off a fossil, strata by strata. Blowing off the dust. Audio archaeology, let's say. Let's say Indiana Jones.

I like to listen to routine take-offs and landings. The pilots sound like performance poets. I picture them crinkled over the control board in black berets, anaemic fingers snapping, clasping espressos, eyes cast to the far corner, too cool for contact, for the stewardess with the pretzels and the can of V8.

Flaps five.

Flaps five.

Flaps one.

Flaps one.

Flaps up.

Say what?

Flaps up.

Flaps up.

―――――

My sister toured once, ten years ago, after her junior year of high school. She hit the major towns on the praise radio circuit. Lubbock, Texas, to Lynchburg, Virginia. "Lynchburg," I had said when she showed me her itinerary. "Lynchburg?"

She shrugged. "They have the world's largest evangelical university."

The tour was eight weeks, to private Christian schools and rodeos. Her merch team sold chastity rings. She brought me home a mug that said *TEAM JESUS* and filled it with prayer jellybeans. Red for the blood you shed. Black for my sinful heart. Yellow for the Heaven above, and so on. I still have them. I think she meant it as a joke.

She died in childbirth. A c-section that led to a blood clot that led to a stroke. We talked on the phone the night before. She told me they had painted the nursery yellow, which the decorator described as String. She said that yellow can be shrill; it's hard to get yellow right. She said she got it right. She said, you know the colour of a wheel of lemon when you hold it to the sun? I said, perfect. Have you settled on name? She said yes. Jaime. Because on paper it reads like *j'aime*.

―――――

Jaime turned four last month. I talked to her on Skype. When she grins she thrusts her chin at you like a goat. I can picture her in a garden this way, neck craned to the sun, as daylilies do, and sunflowers. Heliotropism, I think it's called.

―――――

After lunch, I found Joy Vernon's single on YouTube. The

song is called "Delilah," the video shot at her father's bee farm. She sings against a barn wall in a breezy shirtdress, and she picks her banjo. A low, pinging banjo, against that wall, and her voice is blue and dusky.

Halfway through the video, I felt a brush at my elbow, and I turned to find April the new linguist behind me in her chair. She had wheeled it from her desk across the aisle. I shifted, and she rolled nearer.

"She's lovely, isn't she?" she said when the video ended.

"Yes," I said.

"Could you play the song again?"

I dragged back the play bar. We watched the video from the start. Bees in the wisteria. Joy's hair in her eyes as she bows to see the strings.

"Carrot slice?" said April. She had packed her lunch in a Japanese bento box. Everything compartmentalized. A slot for the chopsticks.

"Thank you." She passed a carrot into my palm. It looked carefully cut. On a diagonal, the edge serrated.

"I used to work in homicides," she said. "Voice ID from emergency phone calls, and so on." We still faced the computer screen—Joy at the barn again, strumming the banjo between verses. "This one case, the vic was an opera singer." She paused to snap her lunchbox. "I never liked opera. But after a week on the case, I ordered her recording of *Evita* online. I listened to the tracks over and over."

I nodded. The YouTube video had ended. April turned to me. Her cheeks looked worn somehow, smooth and unsunned, but as if the skin were pulled too tightly to her ears.

She continued, "When you replay a voice in evidence for eight hours a day, you can almost know them. And when you catch a glimpse of their life before, you get immersed. I get immersed. In the knowing of them."

I stared at her.

She looked down. "Unprofessional, I know."

When she raised her eyes, I was still staring. She held the

eye contact. In that moment, I understood that she understood that I understood everything she said.

———

I often see her at the vending machine. She never buys anything, but she slides her eyes over each item through the glass. I stopped once. When she noticed me, she turned toward the elevator. I said, "too many choices?" and she smiled and waggled her lunch kit.

———

You get into the habit of transcription: sound of smarties dispensed from the machine, sound of coke can, sound of leather soles on a vinyl floor. Sometimes you try to adjust the levels. At the crosswalk, when I race a yellow light. Sound of honk. At home, when the neighbours yell, and one of them unhooks the fire extinguisher. Sometimes my fingers stretch for the mouse.

———

After work today, I returned to the newspaper stand and bought the last fifteen copies of the *Oregonian*. I don't know why. But they were only a dollar each.

———

For Jaime's fourth birthday, I mailed an easy bake oven. She loved it. The cookie dough turns pink. She said to me on Skype, "This present is my number two favourite." But I want to send a gift I didn't find on page one of the Toys "R" Us flyer. Origami, maybe. Her mother loved origami. I have this polaroid of her folding paper cranes—30 of them, for her classmates on Valentine's day instead of cards or cinnamon hearts. Are four year olds into paper?

My sister and I bought ants on television once. *An entire colony, queen included.* We converted our fish tank into a two-story formicarium—poured plaster over a plastic wall, over the clay tunnels we had shaped with our palms. Plus leaves and sand. The leaves you call "forage," plant material for grazing live-stock, a term we adopted. Livestock. Can't play soccer after school—have to check the herd.

She sang for them. I played rhythm: chopsticks on an empty plastic jug. The ants go marching one by one, hurrah, hurrah. Work songs. You could watch them for hours, and sometimes we did. The entire colony shimmering through the chambers, a still black line, though every ant moved. Frames of celluloid projected on a screen, like a river, like blood cells. How motion can be static—it gets you thinking.

When we spotted an ant too close to the cheesecloth, she would fetch petroleum jelly from the bathroom, and we fin-gered streaks of it around the lip of the aquarium. I told her they harvested vaseline from jellyfish.

She said, "Do not."

I said, "Do too," and smeared a daub of it into her bangs.

We later experimented with radio and production speed. Which is to say, crawling. Which is to say, with speakers sit-uated on either side of the formicarium, do ants file faster to the Imperial March or ABBA? The study proved inconclu-sive.

After a couple of months, the plaster moulded and ants found their way into the kitchen, into the paper sack of flour and the dried figs. My mother made me dump the tank in the park, "at least two blocks from our house." My sister started piano. She signed up for voice lessons twice a week with an Italian woman who sang Off-Broadway. I took up coin collection. There was money in coins. Ha, ha.

27

And they all go marching down.
   To the ground.
      To get out of the rain.

———

A quick hello from your cockpit crew, this is flight 166 with service to New York. We'll be flying at 38,000 feet, mostly smooth, for four hours and fifteen minutes takeoff to landing.

———

I've heard the cabin safety announcement so often, I could probably be a flight attendant. In preparation for departure, please be certain your seat back is straightened and your tray table stowed. There are a total of eight exits on this aircraft. Two door exits at the front of the aircraft, four window exits over the wings, and two door exits at the rear of the aircraft. To start the flow of oxygen, reach up and pull the mask toward you. Place the mask over your nose and mouth. Place the elastic band over your head. The plastic bag will not inflate.

———

I have this shirt with a soundboard printed on the front. The caption says, *I know what all these buttons do.* I think a pilot could wear this shirt also.

———

Today, April wears a wool sweater the colour of eggshells, the colour of string. She's hennaed her hair very red. Poppy, I'd say. I think she must attract hummingbirds.

At break, I stopped behind her at the vending machine and watched her scan the items. I don't even think she brought her wallet. I stood there for a full minute before I caught her staring at me through the glass.

She turned. "Go ahead, I'm not in line."

"Me neither," I said.

She shifted her eyes to the potted plant.

"You know they're scented?" I said.

"I'm sorry?"

"The lemons."

She drew her eyes to the yellow baubles of plastic fruit.

"Real wood, too," I continued. "We voted for it last year. They emailed options from a catalogue."

The elevator dinged open and one of the techs from fifth floor strolled out behind us. April stepped for the door. I stepped with her.

"What were the other options?" she said.

"Orange." I walked inside the elevator and leaned against the far wall. "Banana. Bamboo."

"I would have voted bamboo."

The elevator opened at the main floor. I followed her through the lobby into the courtyard, an urban "greenspace" designed with white-slab cement, birch mulch, a stand of honeylocusts and a fountain.

I said, "They described the lemon trees as *evergreen*."

She said, "Well. I don't suppose they lose leaves."

We bought coffees from an espresso bar across the street and carried them back to the fountain—a rectangular pond like a wading pool, with a hunk of granite in the centre for the spout. In fact, I'd seen the fountain used as a wading pool a few times. And as a birdbath. And as a urinal. But such is public art.

I offered her a piece of my croissant—one stuffed with chocolate, so what I said was, "pain au chocolat?"

29

She said, "No thank you."

I sipped my coffee.

She said, "I'm not supposed to have this, but you want to hear?" She outstretched her iPhone, the white wires of earbuds looped around her thumb.

I nodded.

"One of the survivors posted it on YouTube."

She offered me an earbud and plugged the second into her own ear. We bowed over the phone. I could feel the friction of the space between our foreheads. There's a point where technology mimics the past. iPads like slates, like the Flintstones, like chisels. The phone felt divinatory—as if we should be bent over a bowl of water.

She tapped the screen and opened the video. She pressed play.

Rain blew into the camera, diagonal sheets of it into the aluminum and brown water. The camera jolted up and you could see people, their orange life vests, crowded onto the wing. The rear slides had extended. They floated uselessly, like slapstick rubber chickens. What you could hear was shouting—passengers shouting to passengers in the water— *Grab here—Grab my hand*—passengers shouting to passengers to swim away—*Dive—Before it goes*—crew shouting to passengers to stop shouting. What you could hear was rain. Drumming into metal, into hard water, pinging off the life vests. And a continuous chime from the interior of the aircraft, ding ding ding, like your door's open, a friendly reminder before you leave the parking-lot. And there, in the corner of the frame, you could see her treading water. She had floated the furthest from the wreck, her hair starfished out around her shoulders. She drifted further from the plane with every paddle. Her mouth opened and closed, but not in communication, her eyes unfocused, or focused on a distance. She was singing. You could see she was singing.

———

To fold a paper crane, your paper must be square. With sixteen newspapers and scissors from Reception, you can cut a lot of squares. I began with a lifestyles story on the 2002 Miss America. I pressed her face in half. Then I folded the same line onto the reverse side, whitespace for an AT&T ad. I followed a dotted diagram online and ignored all the video how-to's. I don't like to have to pause and rewind.

April found me at 8:30, after she cycled back to work for her phone. I had moved to the floor at this point, to the strips of paper I snipped from the squares. I stored the completed cranes in an emptied recycling box—fired them from where I sat, like paper planes. Paper cranes. Nose first into the box, or onto the surrounding carpet.

When she saw me, she backed up, then stepped forward, then stood very still. "We used newspaper for my guinea pig," she said. "You look like my guinea pig."

"You have a guinea pig?"

"I left my phone."

"Okay."

"When I was twelve." She folded her arms over her ribs. "Her name was Rosa."

She helped me fold cranes. We plugged in her iPhone. We listened to Don't Cry For Me, Argentina on repeat. By midnight, we needed to borrow another recycling box from the lab across the hall. I noticed we both folded A3 so that Joy Vernon's face pointed outward, from the tail of the crane, or the wings.

I think I can fit the cranes into three oversize boxes from UPS. I'll mail the polaroid of my sister with the first parcel. In the photo, she hovers a blue gingham crane above her head. She balances the wings between her fingers like she might let go. Like she knows the crane will stay suspended when she drops her hands.

31

Roadnotes

September 29
Spencer,

I have quit the library and quit town. My plan is to pursue autumn. To track the metamorphosis of deciduous woodlands. Where the leaf turns, there turn I. My first destination: the Laurentians. Mont Tremblant. La Symphonie des Couleurs. Southwest on Highway 40 to Montreal, then the Trans-Canada all the way up. From the Laurentians I will follow the colour south. The Green Mountains of Vermont, the Kancamagus Scenic Byway in New Hampshire, down down down, until pigment leaves the leaves, until winter strips the branches bare.

I have brought: a road map of the United States Eastern Seaboard, the Complete Field Guide to Fall Foliage, and Mom's lime MB roadster, which has not seen asphalt since the third impaired driving charge. She told us if we had two pennies left in the world we should buy a loaf of bread with one and a lily with the other. This is my lily.

Affectionately yours,
Sid

———

October 1
Spence,

Yes, the colours are a symphony. I write from a ski suburb beside Tremblant called Petit Rocher. (I found accommodation outside town because town makes me feel trapped inside a Styrofoam city plan.) We are in what is called the "first wave." The yellow wave. Saffron leaves grope the birches like a thousand rubber gloves. Which reminds me—I found Mom's lambskin gloves on the backseat. The ones that snap at the back of the wrist, that she wore for "Sunday spins" around the countryside. What I remember is she never needed to remove them to count quarters for parking.

After a late lunch I poked around a Tremblant souvenir shop. They sell metal spouts and hand drills for tapping. The romance of the idea overcame me. I bought one of each, then drove for an hour until every tree was a sugar maple. (There is a chapter on tree identification in my Fall Foliage Guide, with leaf silhouettes on the pages like ink blots.) I pulled over and selected a tree close to the road. The instructions said to drill on an incline for the sap to run down, so I did. Then I tapped the spout through the bark with the handle of my drill. I had forgotten to buy a collection pail, so I used my Snapple bottle from lunch. I was crouched nose-to-spout at the foot of the tree, Snapple bottle thrust under the tap, waiting for the thing to leak when I heard a cough. A Hyundai had parked behind the roadster, and inside the Hyundai was a family of three. Their windows were rolled down and they stared from yellow, orange, and red visors. The woman in the passenger's seat (yellow visor) rested her elbow in the window frame and held binoculars. She told me that tapping season begins in February.

The Snapple bottle reminds me of my first and last ballet class, when I needed to bring a water bottle and we didn't have any so Mom sent me to the studio with an empty mickey of gin.

Next stop: Kancamagus Scenic Byway.

From Rocher with Love,
Sid

———

October 3
Spencer,

On the drive to New Hampshire I tried to pinpoint the rupture of Mom's sanity. I couldn't. I think this means either A. she was born a lunatic, or B. wrongly committed. I lean toward A. Thoughts?

Reasons why A:
1. She had an unnatural detachment from loved ones (you, me), and an unnatural attachment to American naturalism (the Helga Series by Andrew Wyeth.)
2. After her alumni lecture at the Art Academy of Cincinnati she burned her collection in the school ceramics kiln (minus the sold self-portrait.)
3. On our drive home from the lecture series we stopped at the Texas Snake Farm and she threatened to kill herself with an asp.
4. She poached eggs in cranberry juice.

I'm in Newport, NH. The centre of town is an opera house, which I think is an idea that should prevail more in urban design.

Had to buy a fresh battery for the roadster in Montreal, but she's purred ever since. Also picked up a copy of the Chronicle-Telegraph and read the obituary. I liked how you began with "Once upon a time."

Living Free Or Dying in New Hampshire,
Sidney

———

34

October 6
Spence,

The Kancamagus Scenic Byway is a three hour drive on a postcard. I arrive with the prologue to the second wave: leaves the colour of canned salmon. Clouds streak the sky like lawn-mower tracks, and the air is warm and thick with the scent of fermented apples. En route to the byway I passed Santa's Village, which is home to an "electroanimated jingle jamboree" and a giraffe-sized drummer boy. Larger-than-life seasonal statuary discomfort me.

Do you remember the December we got the blue spruce? We returned from the ballet and she let me light the bottom candles, but when I stretched for a higher bough my velvet jumper caught fire. You came running and she leaned against her armchair with eyes as grey and cold as nickels. On Christmas morning she cooked ricotta pancakes and poached pears, but for herself only took a cigarette and mulled wine from the night before. And on Boxing Day, she locked herself in the attic with the phonograph and Madama Butterfly, then emerged three afternoons later in her cotton peignoir and walked to the river bank to collect snow drops.

Honestly, Spence? That Christmas I wanted to buy her the asp.

Sidney

————

October 7

I'm sorry I never went to the funeral.

————

35

October 10
Spence,

Happy Thanksgiving. It's nine o'clock and the moon is sickled enough to hang a coat. I'm in Cavendish, Vermont, which is a town entirely unremarkable save for the man with a metal rod in his head. (Phineas Gage. Railroad worker, 1848. Google him.)

Dinner was a can of rice pudding from an AM/PM in Ludlow. The cashier had cream soda breath and Caesar bangs (you know the kind that bisect your forehead like saw teeth?), and when I made him break a twenty he called me a "leaf peeper."

I can count the number of times she hugged us in the last two decades. Twice. Jean-Baptiste Day, 1990: I successfully smoke like a lady. March 1992—you get into her old art school.

Haven't reached mecca yet. (Mecca, for leaf peepers, is the Green Mountains.) I spent the afternoon driving through central Vermont, and skipped the World's Largest Filing Cabinet for a town named Barre (granite capital of America and source for most of the tomb stones.) In Williamstown I toured Knight's Spider Web Farm, which is run by a bald veteran with webs tattooed on his elbows. He cultivates spider webs, then sprays them white and lacquers them onto black boards. This kind of art makes me think that if you stare at the sun long enough you'll see rainbows.

Tomorrow: Mecca. Then New York.

Never moon a werewolf,
Sid

———

October 11
Spencer,

An hour into the Green Mountains I passed a blackcurrant bush and stopped the car in the middle of the road. The berries uneaten by birds were plump and overripe, and I peeled them in clusters from the vine. My lips and nails are violet with juice and it's the closest I've felt to gleefully carnivorous.

Some things I miss:
1. She cut apples width-wise so the core made a star.
2. She wore lipstick and never stained the glass.
3. She saved her watermelon seeds in a jam jar and tried several summers to grow her own patch.
4. She took milk baths.

On my last visit, she didn't speak. Not even when I told her you finished the sunflower series. And when I mentioned I had memorized all hundred divisions of the Dewey Decimal System, she didn't even roll her eyes. You should have come with me.

I'm spending the night in Albany at a pie shop that moonlights as a motor inn. An elephantine Sassafras grows in the parking-lot. We don't have many Sassafras trees up North. Their leaves have broad, rounded lobes that are layered like a wedding cake tall enough to conceal a stripper. I'm going to lay under the boughs and see if I can't get myself entirely buried.

Love Sidney.

I'm in Auburn, NY. There aren't many leaves here, but there are crows, which from a distance look like leaves, especially when you cross your eyes.

There really are a lot of fucking crows. They line the chimneys and telephone wires and the awning of Curley's Restaurant opposite my window. The concierge says they arrived early this year. Every autumn since 1993, a murder of 50,000 to 70,000 crows descends upon the ancient Aboriginal burial ground and proceeds to the town centre to roost.

They remind me of the baby crow Mom saved after Jacques-Joseph shot its mother with a pellet gun. Do you remember how she wanted to teach it to speak, so she clipped the tongue, and then it couldn't eat and starved to death? I think that incident neatly paraphrases our childhood.

The crows look finest when they fly. They take wing en masse and sweep through air like a handheld fan. And when you bend your neck back to see only up, the sky looks like paper that a child has spattered with ink. The town hates them. They tear apart dumpsters and caw 'til the cows come home. And apparently by winter the volume of excrement is a biohazard. But I think they're magnificent.

She always wanted to move back to Ohio. Does it give her too much credit to believe we stayed in Quebec because she didn't want to uproot us? I think we should have tried harder for the health centre in Maine.

Guess what? The U.S. Department of Agriculture has activated a Fall Foliage Hotline. 1-800-354-4595. An automated voice informs callers of the country's colour peaks. The leaves in the New York and Pennsylvania Allegheny Forest should be exquisite. I head there tomorrow.

Unique New York Unique New York,
Sidney

October 15

Remember the lightning storm that summer we camped on Kipawa Lake? Before the trees burned down, they were backlit by this glorious blaze. The trunks loomed scarlet and the colours were divine. Well the sun glows behind the hickory trees as I write and the likeness is striking.

Are you familiar with the botany behind fall foliage change? In late summer the leaf's base develops a layer of cork that plugs its veins and prevents the entrance of moisture and minerals. Our symphonie des couleurs is a tree weaning its leaves off water.

Two weeks tomorrow is your opening. I hate myself for missing it. Good luck. Remember the liquor license. Don't be nervous. The collectors will line around the block.

Your Sidster (Ha ha ha)

PS—I think she was the most beautiful woman in the world. I think this is what redeemed her. She lived by a wild, unreasoned, breathless devotion to beauty. And not just her own.

PPS—My contact with humanity has officially reduced to you and muffler men.

Oct. 17

The bitch stole my boots! The pearl-coloured full-quill ostrich skin Tony Lamas I won from the Montreal Gazette's "Wild West" poetry contest in 1986! The pearl-coloured full-quill ostrich skin Tony Lamas that vanished a month later, that I scoured the house for until the hardwood bruised my knees, that I just found in the original box underneath the passenger seat when I reached to find my fallen crust of pizza.

I am parked on the William Flynn Highway, outside the Store Shaped Like a Stealth Bomber, and I'm fuming in both French and English translations of the word. Will write more in Pittsburgh.

In Pittsburgh. I think the worst thing about our mother was the way she looked at us. She watched her children as she might a painting. Like she wasn't expecting us to stare back at her. And worse still, she watched us as her own painting. We failed because she was venomously self-critical. And worse than that, we failed because she did not craft us. You and I were the dice that spilled from chromosome Yahtzee, and how could that compare with Tarbell's Mother and Child in a Boat?

At least you went to art school. I think my decision to stack books for a living prompted her second relapse.

Tomorrow I try my luck in Tennessee.

Don't be bashful, Nashville.
Sidney

———

October 18
Spence,

I opened the trunk. Which is to say I spent two weeks in our dead mother's car without opening the trunk, until three hours ago. I was "booting it" (they still fit) down the Pennsylvania Turnpike when the roadster met its ninth hole and burst its first tire. ("Pennsylvania: where winter eases driving because the potholes fill with snow.") I popped the back for a spare and found my: velvet riding helmet, patent leather Mary Janes, scarlet beret, flower press. Your: rock collection, private school blazer, clarinet, kaleidoscope. The buck antlers you found up North, a tambourine, and what looks to be the fourth floor of my Victorian doll house.

The roadster's at Esso getting refurbished. I've decided to spend a second night in Pittsburgh.

Sidney

———

October 19
Spencer,

After two cups of Jasmine tea, a bowl of won ton soup, and three hours inside an infinity of crimson dots, I'm going to Cincinnati. (In regards to the third point—there's an Infinity Dots installation at the Pittsburgh Mattress Factory.) No more bashful Nashville, no Tennessee Waltz; it's tin soldiers and Nixon on the I-70 to Ohio. I write from a hoisin smeared booth at Lai Fu Restaurant, waiting for the bill and picking cabbage from my teeth with the fork my waiter gave me when he saw my attempt at chopsticks.

Do you think it's naive to believe her theft of our treasured childhood items implies a maternal sentimentality?

The bill's here. John Ruskin is inside my fortune cookie. I don't know what's odder—the quote's relevance to my travels, or the fact that an English art critic has replaced Confucius.

"Remember that the most beautiful things in the world are the most useless; peacocks and lilies, for example."

Sid

———

41

October 20
Spencer,

On the road to Cincinnati I passed three sunflower fields with flowers oily and yellow and spread-eagle beneath the sun, and then I passed a dead sunflower field, their heads bowed to the dirt like burnt out street lamps. (This fourth field would make a great finale to your set.) I passed a manor with a chimney and eaves that bled Virginia Creeper, and then I passed the World's Largest Amish Buggy, and the World's Largest Horseshoe Crab, and the World's Largest Apple Basket, and the World's Largest Washboard, and the World's Largest Crystal Ball, and the World's Largest Gavel, and the World's Largest Mortarboard Graduation Cap, and an animatronic Smokey the Bear. I alighted from the roadster at a chestnut tree near Lancaster and collected nuts in the front of my sweater. Then I stopped for coffee and a slice of cherry pie at a rest stop a few hundred metres away. But they didn't have cherry pie so I ordered coleslaw and a burger, and the trucker on the stool to my left told me that what I collected were Buckeye nuts, not Chestnuts, and what I stopped at was a Buckeye Tree, the state tree of Ohio.

I spent last night at a Comfort Inn Over-the-Rhine. I aimed to be at the Academy of Art by now, but instead I'm on my third paper cup of coffee. What if they don't remember her? What if they have no clue?

Continued:

I met the academy dean who sent me to the curator of the Childlaw Gallery who sent me to the curator of the Pearlman Gallery who told the student at the welcome desk to type something into a computer. So now I have an address for the patron who bought Mom's self portrait, which struck me as a breech of privacy, but it's amazing how far you'll get with the right driver's license and a death certificate. Our patron is "Ms. Izobel Moss" of Jerseyville, Illinois.

So. To Illinois.

———

October 22
Spencer,

Five hours and the state of Indiana after my last letter, I pulled into a driveway littered with autobodies, a mile or so outside Jerseyville. At the end of the drive was a house the colour of a recycling bin. It looked freshly painted and under the sun gave the impression of melting. A chain link fence enclosed a leafless pear tree, a plastic kiddie pool the same wet blue as the house, and a two-legged picnic bench angled between dirt and sky like a seesaw. A woman with three arms emerged from behind the tree. One swung against her hip as she walked into the shade of the trunk, the second was bent 90 degrees and perpendicular to the ground, and a third budded from that one like a flexed lobster claw. I asked if her name was Izobel Moss, and when she stepped from the shadow her claw became an owl. A midsized owl the height of my forearm, with plumage like tweed and a chain that tethered him to the woman's wrist. She said, "who wants to know," which felt so Hollywood that I said I had the ruby slippers and she said, "Well that's a horse of a different colour. Come on in."

Except that didn't happen. She said, "who wants to know" and I didn't reply right away because she stood at the tip of the tree's shadow on the grass and really, really resembled its crowning Christmas ornament. Then the owl raised his wings and flapped, and flew the length of the chain and flapped, and hung suspended in the air like a helium balloon, and I said, "Sidney Marion. I think you bought my mother's painting.

43

The self-portrait. She died a few weeks ago, and I wondered if I might see it." She didn't respond so I offered to show her the death certificate but she said "no need" and led me into her house.

And there she was. Our mother. In her ankle length sealskin coat. You paint like her, you know. In the portrait, she wears a cloche hat, but her hair is slung over her shoulders, the ends corkscrewed and long enough to be stuffed into the coat pockets. I remember those pockets were deep enough to fit hardcover books and tins of licorice. Mom painted her skin pale except for the cheeks, which look rouged from the cold or physical exertion. Her eyes are cast toward the unopened umbrella she clutches with both hands, and her lips press together as if to keep from laughing. The portrait is exactly how I wish I could remember her.

I went back outside where Izobel and her owl waited for me on the porch, and without any sort of premeditation I asked to buy the painting. I hadn't planned to buy it. I didn't think I wanted to. I'm sure I didn't want to. She said it wasn't for sale. I said, "I'll pay you double." She said, "I don't need the money," and I said, "But she's my mother!" Then the only sound was the chortling of the owl. Izobel's eyes washed over me and she rotated the metal cuff from the chain around her forearm until her stare settled at my feet. "What size are your boots?"

Bitch steals my boots even from the grave.

I called the foliage hotline last week—reports for the Mark Twain National Forest look optimistic. I operate the gas in my socks because I can't find the shoes I brought with me. Mom rides shotgun.

Sid

———

44

October 24
Spencer,

Mark Twain did not disappoint. Missouri's reached the Third Wave. Sweetgum and Oak, Black Tupelo and Elm: they all look dipped in ketchup.

Last night I bought three quarts of milk from the Hazelwood Grocery. I didn't know the optimum fat percentage for milk baths, so I got one carton of skim, one 2%, and one homogenized. I filled the tub with milk and hot water and rose hips I picked from the wild bush behind the motel. Now my skin is silk and I feel like Marie Antoinette, or Cleopatra, or our Mother.

I miss you, Spence. If I leave tomorrow I can be home for your opening. The Lost Maples of Texas will still be there next fall. And Mom would look fine in your studio.

Time to get my drive on Route 55.

Love Sidney.

KEVIN COUTURE

How to Rescue a Bear Cub

I. GET THE FACTS.

Mom says, "There's a stray cub in the acreages. Tom Foster's dog chased the sow away and now the simpleton's been feeding the damn thing—bread soaked in apple juice. *Stay away from there. Understand?*" Dad shifts his pipe to the side and says, "She's right. Listen to your mother." And later when I tell him, my friend Jude says, "No way. A bear? What the hell are we waiting for?"

2. GATHER MATERIALS.

Jude lives with his father. His Dad's a carpenter but he's been out of work a while, lost his job after Jude's Mom—also a carpenter—took off. Their yard is filled with odd cuts of wood, chicken wire, old tools, bottles. We collect the supplies we'll need and go inside for lunch. Jude's Dad is at the pub so Jude makes us mayonnaise sandwiches with Cheezies; he doesn't wipe the counter before or after. We discuss strategy while we eat. Jude calls the cub, *little fucker*, and refers to Tom Foster as *the retard*. My sandwich, I notice, tastes like sour milk.

3. BUILD A TRAP.

My role in the construction is *holder* and *go-fer* because Jude's better with tools. He sweats and sticks his tongue out while he concentrates. I ask him if his parents taught him how to build and he stops mid-cut and stares at me for a whole minute. Pretty soon though we've got a bear box: plywood sides and a small wire window in front. It's good. Really good, and I go to high-five Jude but he's busy looking out the front door. Then he goes in the other room and makes a phone call. "Can you check again?" I hear him say. And a minute later, "Yeah, whatever."

4. ENLIST REINFORCEMENTS.

"Think about it," Jude says. "You'll be a hero." Tom Foster stares at us. He lives in a double-wide inherited from his folks, has a worker who checks on him regularly, pays for things with his government cheque. He and his dog, Hovercraft, inspect the trap like it's some kind of a landmine. We tell him his truck can transport the bear to the dump afterwards, where all the other bears are. "Where the mother is, probably," I add and for some reason, I look at Jude. Tom rubs his chin for a long, long time, his forehead wrinkled as a curtain. Finally, he agrees. "Okay then," he says. "If you guys say so."

5. SET UP.

We dump some bread in a bucket. Add apple juice, honey, and raspberry jam. We put the bucket in the box, and the box in the overgrown orchard. When it's done, Jude asks Tom if he can use the phone. "There is no phone," Tom says. He smiles and leans forward to let his dog lick his teeth. At first I'm worried Jude might crack him in the head while he's down there, bust a window or something. (He doesn't take well to disappointment.) Instead, he sits on the sofa and mumbles to himself. I listen, but all I can make out is: *should have left a note, fuck it anyway,* and *why should I care?*

6. EXECUTE THE PLAN.

We wait. Tom feeds us Pic-a-Pop and dry crackers while Hovercraft sucks up floor-crumbs. At one point, Tom wants to play cards but Jude gives him a look so he sits there and whistles instead. After a while, Tom asks, "Do your Moms and Dads know where you are?" and the room goes silent, like it's been instantly filled with dirt. Before we can answer or think too much about it though, Jude stands up and points out the window—a small, black shape is wobbling toward the box. "Little fucker," Jude whispers. "And...also...*Holy shit.*" The dog starts to growl.

7. TAKE ACTION.

"Come on," Jude says. He steps onto the porch, staring at the woods beyond the orchard while Tom holds the dog back. The cub is much smaller than I imagined, like a stuffed toy standing next to the box. I want to say that to Jude but he's way too focused, keeping his eyes on the edge of the forest. Suddenly Hovercraft barks; the cub runs into the trap and the door shuts tight behind it. It works! It actually works! But instead of celebrating, Jude picks up a stick and yells, "Goddamn it." He starts running and when it's too late to turn back, Tom and I finally see what he sees: the mother bear, lumbering toward him from the depths of the trees.

8. RECONSIDER THE SITUATION.

The sow makes a huffing sound, deep and menacing, an earthquake of a noise. Jude doesn't stop though. For some reason he goes over to the trap and tries to open it with the stick. The mother stands on its hind legs and bellows, starts moving faster, but the door to the trap is stuck. Jude begins hitting the box with his hands. Tearing at the wood, poking his fingers through the gaps in the wire. The cub screams like a child with a smashed thumb. Tom closes his eyes. The bear is almost there. A couple more steps. And I don't know what to do.

9. SWITCH TO PLAN B.

We don't have a Plan B. And the bear is nearly on top of Jude. "Should we release the dog?" I say to Tom, whose eyes are still closed. "Don't release the dog," Jude yells. I try to free Hovercraft anyway but Tom's hands are too strong and the dog is going crazy. The bear stops in front of Jude and roars, the cub is screaming too. I yank the collar one last time and finally the dog comes free. He races toward the bear and when he gets there, the sow backs off for a moment. But then she takes a swipe and the dog tumbles, head over heels. "Hovercraft!" Tom yells. The bear keeps coming.

10. HOPE FOR INTERVENTION.

My parents only take me to church for three things: Easter, Christmas, and the weddings of people they know. Still, for some reason I fold my hands, look up to the sky, and get ready to pray. At that instant though, before I even get started, headlights appear and my parents' truck races up beside the house. The sow stares at Jude for a few seconds with the lights shining right on her, making decisions. Then she turns and runs off and Jude screams, "Wait! Come back, *please.*" But he still can't open the box. Tom runs over to his dog and picks him up. My parents get out along with Jude's dad and they rush over too. The cub stops yelling. Jude falls to his knees, buries his face in his hands. And the mother bear disappears into the forest.

I don't see Jude for a few days. When I do, he's walking by the bus station, carrying a suitcase and eating a chocolate bar. "Hey," I say. But he just stares at me and continues on. At first I want to rush home and tell my folks about him, make a phone call, tell *someone*. But in the end I stand there and do nothing. When everyone arrived that night with the bear, my parents hugged me and wiped away tears; Tom tended to Hovercraft, bandaging up his injured leg; and Jude's dad smacked him in the back of the head and said, "You fuck-up. You know, you're the reason...." Then he and my father dismantled the box and freed the cub. We watched it run off in the direction the mother went, more or less, and we climbed into the truck to go home. As we drove away, Tom Foster waved goodbye to us from the porch and I wondered what his parents were like when they were around. He was sitting quietly on his steps, rocking back and forth, holding his dog and singing to it as if it was a small child. As if it was a present, something precious. All he had in the whole entire world.

The Mimic

When I bothered to think about it, which wasn't often, I imagined my father's home as flawless and pristine. A post-card house with geometric hedges around the perimeter, a perfectly cut lawn, windows reflecting the sun in bright, musical, hallelujah rays. Nothing around anywhere that might sully up the place or disrupt the ideal life he'd been having on his own. But the house I'm looking at now, the one right in front of me, is nothing like that at all.

I pull off to the side and take it all in, listening to the tick of the car's engine. There's a broken fence spanning one edge of the property and an overgrown spruce along the other, its lower branches hacked away to create a small, passable tunnel to the backyard. In front lay a flower bed filled with knap-weeds, thistles, piles of firewood neglected so long they've gone to rot. Then there's the building itself: a brown bunga-low with brown trim, brown stairs and brown curtains in every tightly shut window. It looks like a flophouse or an abandoned hideout, a guilty place. But I didn't come here to judge.

"Helloo-oo! You must be Dierk's daughter. Wait there. I'll come over," someone says. It's the neighbour, Rita. I recognize her voice from the phone, the pitch high and sharp like the ping of a barcode scanner. She's a large woman, the type who's only comfortable wearing those shapeless, cotton muumuu dresses. The one she's in now has Eiffel Towers and French poodles all over it and when she gets close, I can smell the baby powder she uses to keep her flesh from rubbing together.

"Hello," I say. "I'm Elena Werden."

"Pleased to meet you." At first Rita offers a big smile along with her hand but then she remembers why I'm here and low-ers her eyes. "Sorry for your loss," she says. "I've got the keys right here."

She hands them to me and stands there, breathing. Waiting for me to ask about my father's last days. Perhaps decide on the future of the house or explain why I've never visited before though my father's lived here for decades.

"Thank you," I say. "This should only take a few days. I'll be in touch if legal arrangements require." I put the keys in my pocket and turn to get the supplies out of the car. I move slowly, giving Rita plenty of time to leave. She's still there though. Studying me like the eyes of a painting.

"Is there something else?" I ask, turning back to face her.

"Oh. Yes, well, there's the matter of the bird, of course."

I stare at her, blankly.

"Your father's parrot. It must have slipped your mind with everything that's been going on, you poor thing. Don't worry. I'll wait until you're settled before bringing him over."

"Fine," I tell her. "That'll be just fine."

Fifteen minutes after the conversation at the car, Rita brings over the parrot I knew nothing about. How could I know? I haven't spoken to my father since the day he left, back when I was nine years old. My mother refused to talk about him after he was gone, saying it had no purpose. "There's no sense in stirring things up, now is there, Elena?" she told me. "Just block it out. You'll get used to it soon enough."

And she kept her silence right up until the day she passed, five years ago from pancreatic cancer. She shouldn't have worried about my *blocking things out* though. There was nothing to block—the only correspondence I received from my father in all those years came last month, his official death certificate and will. Not that it upset me mind you, being fatherless as a child. I was independent enough even then and his leaving only helped nurture that trait, helped turn me into who I am today. Really, if anything, I should have thanked him.

I help Rita carry the blanket-covered birdcage to a corner of the living-room with Plexiglas on the walls, presumably for mess control. We manoeuvre the stand into the flattened circle on the rug and step back to look. A threadbare armchair sits to the left of the cage; behind it, a stack of newspapers. There's a remote lying on an ottoman, a TV on a silver base, and a tin-metal dinner tray standing at the ready. That's it. Nothing else to speak of. It's a dingy place with poor lighting and heavy air, the smell of an oily basement.

"Here's the food," Rita says, putting a bag of seeds on the floor and rubbing some dust off her hands. She looks nervous, like she's selling me an appliance that doesn't work. "He's an African Grey and his name is Lowen. That's all I know. If you need anything else, just call me. I'm always around, dear."

"Thank you," I say, guiding her toward the door before she starts hinting at afternoon tea or some other cordial absurdity. And as soon as she's gone, I finish unpacking.

I set everything out on the table: paper shredder, the local phone book, laptop, a guide called *Duties of an Executor and Trustee.* Then I tape three garbage bags to the edge and label them *goodwill, trash,* and *recycling.* It seems obsessive I know but the more organized I am, the faster this will go. There are no feelings here to slow me down. No relishing of fond memories. I'd have the same level of connection scorekeeping a game of darts between two drunken strangers. And that's just fine by me.

Suddenly I hear a noise coming from the cage. The parrot is stirring.

I pull the cover off and Lowen stares at me from behind the bars. He's shabby and unkempt. A big grey mess. There are long patches of missing feathers on his body and if he wasn't the only animal in the room, I'd think he was being picked on. I bend down to get a better view, to see what sort of complication I'm forced to deal with here, and the bird looks me up and down like a border guard. As if he's actually sizing *me* up.

"What am I going to do with you?" I say, flicking my nail against the cage and staring into the animal's beady little eyes.

He opens his beak wide enough to house a nectarine.

"Awwwk. What are we going to do, Lowen? What are we going to do now?" he says.

I step back and my skin goes cold, the chill piercing the centre of my bones. Even though it's been a long time, there's no mistaking it: the voice I hear coming from the cage—tone, accent, everything—is the absolute, exact, carbon-copy of my father's.

Just before bedtime, I put on some gloves to feed and water the ridiculous bird. He doesn't say anything else, thank God. Not even a squawk. Lowen is extremely wary of me, as I am of him, and we basically ignore each other the whole time. Precisely the way it should be.

After picking at his food for a while, lethargically, as if he was sorting through floor-sweepings, the bird finally settles in for the night; I do the same, rolling my sleeping bag and pillow out on my father's couch. As soon as I lie down though, I see water stains on the ceiling and splatters on the light fixture from a lousy paint job. It makes me want to scream so I close my eyes and try to block out the whole sickly mess. I think about happier things: my job, decent takeout, my nice organized apartment in the city. Eventually, I feel the tension in my jaw begin to relax. My neck muscles, loosening.

I must be exhausted because I actually start to drift off. The ghostly images of dream take over and I'm too tired to fight them. I let myself glide along, carried like a child from the backseat of a car. Floating safely through doors, up stairs, into a fresh warm bed. It's pleasant, almost musical. And it feels a bit like forgetting. I lose all track of time in the dream and I'm not exactly sure what year it's supposed to be. Then, out of nowhere, I hear a voice. A whispering. The soft noise of someone crying.

"Elena," the voice says, calling me. "Elena."

I sit up, suddenly wide awake. The sound isn't coming from my dream—it's my father's voice here in the room. I'm not stupid, I know it's only the bird but still, it affects me just the same.

I hold my breath and stay perfectly still so I can hear things more clearly, out of curiosity of course. It's completely quiet now though, both inside the house and out. There's not even any traffic noise on the street. A ticking clock. Nothing. And this place has a way of making the silence seem more powerful than it really is.

A few minutes later, Lowen starts up again, filling the room with that familiar voice. I let it wash over me and my skin tingles from the coldness in the air. Then the voice gets louder, more precise, distinguishable. And my cheeks fill with blood as I realize it's not Elena he's been saying after all. It's *Eva*, a name I haven't heard associated with my father ever before. Not in the will, not from Mother, not anywhere.

It continues on long into the night, so softly it's almost inaudible.

"Eva, Eva, Eva."

By ten the next morning I've filled three bags with garbage and one with recycling. I find some official documents in a drawer and put them in a pile for later; everything else I shred with the efficiency and single-mindedness of an ant colony. I don't stop to read anything. Don't ponder the items my father collected over the years. And although I'm slightly curious, Lowen's weirdness last night changes nothing. In fact it all seems kind of stupid here in the light of day.

After what I deem as a sufficient amount of progress has been made, I sit down at the table with the laptop to eat my lunch. And while I'm at it, I make a list of some of the larger items in the house—the uncomfortable couch, the TV, the table and chairs—and enter their descriptions into Craigslist. Then I scroll down and click on the pets section. *African Grey. Complete with own cage and food. Make an offer.*

Lowen comes to life, running his beak back and forth against the bars like a tin cup. It's a coincidence of course but it makes me feel guilty just the same. There's nothing personal in all this though; divesting an estate means just that. Nothing more, nothing less.

Lowen turns his back to me. I hit *enter* and move on.

Thankfully, I have an appointment set up with a realtor this afternoon; going through my father's debris is like trying to swim in a pool of drycleaner bags. I gather the will, the property title, and the encumbrance certificate and put them in a folder titled, *Residence.* I don't see anything else here essential to the listing and I'm about to move on when I spy something hidden between the pages of a bank statement: an old life insurance certificate, the policyholder, not surprisingly, being my father.

It's one of those no-medical-exam-TV-infomercial things written in simple language with a pittance for a payout. The name of the beneficiary, however, has been scribbled over in ink. Crossed off so vigorously the paper's actually torn from the force of the pen. I smooth it out as best I can and hold it up to the light. Only the first name is legible and—although there's no reason to feel this way—I get a little jolt when I notice it's not me. The name, instead, is the same one as last night, the one Lowen was whispering over and over. The enigmatic and increasingly annoying *Eva.*

I have four distinct memories of my father. The first: my sixth birthday. My mother took pictures while Father held the cake. "You missed a candle, darling," he told me, though in reality I hadn't. "See here, Elena? Look close. A little closer." What's memorable is it was the first time I realized my father had an accent. I'd been so used to hearing his German frankness, the crisp pop of syllables, that I hadn't thought much about it before. The candle smoke wisped between us, disguising the mischievous grin on my father's face. And though I knew exactly what he was up to I couldn't stop staring at his mouth, waiting for the next word to come out. I stayed like that, fixated on his lips, until he pushed the cake right into my nose. Rubbed icing all over my tiny face.

The second memory: Darden Lake. Walking out on *Grandmother's Arms*, the fallen, floating tree that had been there forever. There were branches coated in gelatinous moss stretching underwater in every direction. The wood was slick; the lake, clear and deep. "Go ahead. I'm watching," Father said. He was already at the far end of the tree, his hands reaching out to urge me on. I knew I was going to fall even before I took my first step. What I didn't know is whether or not I'd hit my head, end up trapped under a branch, sink like a stone. And when I looked to my father for reassurance, for the life of me I couldn't tell if he'd dive in after me or not. If he'd actually be there to save me.

The third: my father sitting on the porch watching a thunder storm at night. It was a month before the divorce and he'd been sitting there a lot. I went outside to join him and the sudden clack of the screen door startled us both. "Come, Elena," he said. "Sit with me for a while." The rain was loud on the corrugated roof; it ran off the grooves in steady streams like thin steel bars. I climbed on the bench next to him, smelled chewing tobacco on his breath, spiced apples and new leather. He was warm despite the coolness in the air and his body heat kept me from shivering. I remember a lot of lightning that night. The sadness, lit up on my father's face with every blue-white strike of it.

The final memory: the day my father left. I watched from the upstairs window as he put his things in the truck. He wandered back and forth like a bug in a pail. Then he stood in the driveway, thinking for a long time. Mother was at the kitchen table with a cup of coffee, pretending to read a newspaper. Finally, my father came in and I heard him plead with her. He wanted to say goodbye to me but Mother refused. "You want to go? Then go," she screamed. "We'll get used to it before you even shut the door!" I heard her cup smash on the floor, the stark resolution in her voice. And even though I knew it would break my father's heart, I copied her.

Yelling the very same thing from upstairs, from the door of my tiny bedroom.

I call the life insurance company but they find no evidence of that policy number. "It's likely been cancelled," the man says. "We purge records on all defunct policies every five years. Sorry."

The document whines as it goes through the shredder. And then everything's quiet.

I lift the cover off Lowen's cage and he shuffles over and squawks, opening his beak to reveal a squat tongue the colour of dryer lint. I completely ignore him. Instead, I try to imagine what my father looked like before he died. It's funny, I can picture him as he was when I was nine but I can't extrapolate. Can't get a fix on how he must have changed over the years.

"Not that I care, but what *were* you doing all this time, Dierk?" I whisper to myself.

Lowen drops to the floor of the cage and begins hitting his head against the bars. After a while, he curls into a ball, making some sort of avian-moaning sound. I stand there watching him for a long time, mesmerized. Then I realize I'm late for my appointment with the realtor.

I race around and grab my jacket, my purse, and scoop up all the documents I need. And when I finally get the door, I hear Lowen's voice again.

"Goodbye?" he says, quietly. "Goodbye?"

The idiocy of it makes me laugh. "Get used to it," I tell him. And I exit the soon-to-be-on-the-market house, shutting the door behind me harder than I probably need to.

"Helloo-oo!" Rita calls from the other side of the fence. She's watering a flower bed with one of those long wands, wearing a white hat and a pair of sunglasses big enough to shield the space shuttle during re-entry. "How are you coping, dear? Is there anything I can do?"

"Everything's under control. I'm just running late for an

appointment."

"Oh, well. Off you go, then." She gestures toward the car with the sprinkler.

"Actually Rita, I do have a question."

"Yes?"

"Do you know someone named Eva? Connected to my father, I mean?"

She takes off her huge glasses and taps them on her chest, thinking. "No, Deary. No-one I know of," she says, looking around her nice but unremarkable garden.

"And do you recall seeing any guests over here? Maybe someone you didn't know?"

"No, no. Nothing like that. Dierk kept to himself for the most part. Other than Lowen, your father was pretty much alone the whole five years I've been here. It's strange, isn't it? Being all alone. You don't suppose he actually liked it that way, do you?"

The realtor is a guy named Stephen with obviously dyed hair who also knows nothing about my father. He's more than happy to take on the job of selling the house though. I sign a contract instructing him to put it on the market at whatever price he sees fit. A realtor's dream. *Sell the house. Take the first offer. Don't worry about haggling. Just get rid of it.* Clients like me don't come around very often and Stephen is smiling so enthusiastically I can count every single filling in his mouth.

"It shouldn't take long," he tells me as we finish things up. "People are always looking for a good starter place."

"Thank you," I say.

He guides me toward the door and hands me a folder of documents with his business card stapled to the front. "And if there's anything else I can do for you, anything at all, just let me know," he says.

The first thing that comes to mind is asking him if he knows anyone in town named *Eva*. But saying that over and over is starting to sound a little crazy. "That'll do, thank you,"

I say. And then as a joke, I add, "Unless of course you want to adopt a parrot."

"Oh," he replies, his big smile suddenly disappearing. "That's a tough one. How's it doing?"

"I don't know, it's a bird. What do you mean?"

"Well, my aunt had a parrot years ago and they're sort of in it for life. When she died, her bird started freaking out, wouldn't eat, kept chewing at himself," he says. "In fact, as I recall, the parrot only lasted a couple of months before he expired too. The vet said the poor animal just couldn't figure out how to handle grief."

I stare at him for a long time, totally silent. And then Stephen gets this worried look on his face like he's on the verge of losing his commission.

"But hey, I'm just a small-town realtor," he says, patting me on the back. "What the hell do I know about these things?"

For some reason, I'm anxious as I head back to my father's house even though Stephen, as he rightfully implied, was way off base. His aunt was a million years old and her parrot more likely died from second-hand smoke or eating its dinner off of Styrofoam meat trays than anything else. That's the bottom line here and I keep telling myself that the entire drive. Lowen—even though I don't care one way or the other—is going to be just fine.

When I finally get there, I stumble out of the car and drop the realtor's booklet in the driveway. Thankfully though, Rita's not in her yard this time, waving her big hand and *hel-loo-oo-ing* me all the way to the nuthouse. I gather everything up, compose myself, and enter the house.

The phone rings as soon as I get inside, making my heart pound again. "Who's calling please?" I ask.

"Oh, hi. I'm just inquiring about your ad, about the African Grey," the voice says.

"Yes?"

"Well, I wonder if I could see him. Is there a good time for you?"

I look over at Lowen. He's lying on the floor of the cage, his head resting on a patchy, outstretched wing like a leper. He's completely motionless. Stiff-looking. And it doesn't really seem like he's breathing anymore.

"I'm sorry," I tell the man on the phone. "The bird's been sold."

"Oh, that's too bad. I was hoping...."

I hang up and drop the phone on the table. Then I stand there for a while, coming up with excuses. When I can't take it any longer, I walk over to the cage and begin tapping on the bars. Once. Twice. Six times. Finally, Lowen lifts his head and looks up at me. And I release the breath I didn't even know I was holding.

I bend down to get a better look and as soon as my face gets close to the cage, Lowen stands and walks toward me, seemingly okay again. At first, I'm relieved. But then it makes me angry, like someone just pulled a fast one on me. Like I'm being laughed at, led by the nose to some kind of ultimate failure. And for some reason, even though it's crazy, I get the impression this whole episode—the sick bird, Rita the judgemental neighbour, the life insurance debacle, maybe even my father's death itself—is the fault of one person and one person only. Eva, the deceitful, behind-the-scenes, stay-in-the-shadows witch.

"Okay bird," I say. "No more games."

He looks at me with one eye but doesn't respond.

"Tell me who Eva is."

He climbs up the cage, sits on his wooden bar.

"Eva and Dierk." I say slowly. "E-v-a and D-i-e-r-k."

Nothing.

"Eva. Eva. *Eva*," I say, struggling to keep my voice at an acceptable level.

Finally, he reacts. "Beautiful," he tells me, softly. "My beautiful, beautiful girl."

I close my eyes. Not only do I hear my father's voice but I see him in my mind as well, the physical words spilling from his lips. I can feel his fingers on my cheek, smell the tobacco in his shirt. I picture it all and for some reason it stings.

Out of the blue I say, "I'm Elena, Dierk's daughter. Is that who you mean?"

Lowen stares back at me vacantly. His eyes are far away like I don't even exist to him at all. And suddenly I feel very stupid.

What am I doing? He's just an animal, a parrot, *a mimic* for Christ's sake. He doesn't give answers, he does impersonations. And another thing comes to mind: the realization I haven't yet visited the cemetery where my father's remains are buried. Like that has any relevance here at all.

"You think I care?" I yell at Lowen through the bars, holding the cage like you would a child's shoulders. "I don't want your charity, I just want a name, that's all. Goddamn it, Eva, what is your last name?"

And then it hits me.

I run to the laptop and type in *Werden, Eva*. I refine the search with the name of my father's town and, on a hunch, I add *announcements*.

In the archives of the local paper I find this:

Dierk and Eva Werden (nee Cooper) celebrated their undying love for one another on Saturday, July 28th, 2001 in a quiet ceremony at the couple's home in Merritt, British Columbia. A celebration of new beginnings, a connection of two lives. And the everlasting promise of forever.

I also find this:

Eva Werden (nee Cooper) entered into rest suddenly at Merritt, BC on Tuesday, July 11th, 2006. She leaves behind a loving and devoted husband, Dierk Werden, and brother, Jake Cooper of Auckland, New Zealand. Funeral services will be held Saturday, 2:15, at The Church of St Nicholas. She will be dearly missed and never forgotten.

"Got you," I say.

And then, inexplicably, I feel tears running down my cheeks. They just won't stop no matter what I do. It's hard to breathe, my shoulders are actually shuddering with the force of it all. And my stomach, my heart, every inch of me, feels like a towel that had been twisted for a long time and has now, suddenly, been released.

"My God, get it together, Elena," I tell myself, wiping my face as hard as I can. "This is none of your business. You have your own life, a good one, and this is just another irrelevancy in it. Move on. Get it together. You'll get used to it soon enough."

The second I stop talking, Lowen says something as well. He keeps mumbling it over and over like a madman. I don't know why, but it seems important that I know what he's saying. And without thinking, I walk over to the cage, open the door, and put my hand in.

At first he just sits there, snapping his beak like a pair of pruning shears. But then, bit by bit, he sidles over and steps onto my wrist. He's heavier than I imagined, his grip tight on my arm. I lift him out of the cage and bring him close so his face is next to mine, right beside my ear. I feel the heat of his breath on my skin. His beak, smooth as a shell.

And he starts to speak.

"Got you," he whispers.

"What? I...I don't...."

"Get it together, Elena," he goes on. "Get used to it. Get it together. Get used to it."

The words are clear and decipherable, very plain. But it's not my father's voice I hear this time. *It's mine.* He's using my voice now. Except his version is all wrong. His version sounds desperate and bitter and lonely. I'm not any of those things.

I kneel down on the carpet, overwhelmed with something I can't describe, and Lowen hops off my arm and walks a few feet away. He's standing beside my father's chair now, looking up at the empty seat, tilting his head from side to side. Everything around us is quiet but it doesn't feel particularly peaceful, it feels like being smothered. And suddenly, all I want to do is pick Lowen up again, feel his warmth, breathe the same air that he's breathing, have an actual conversation.

But that doesn't make sense. Nothing about this makes any sense at all.

Lowen flaps his wings. He turns away from the chair and takes a single step toward me.

"Say something," I whisper, holding my hands out toward him, urging him on. "Please. Please. Say something else."

Lemonade Free

There's a kid with a lemonade stand down the block from the meeting house. Little toothpick umbrellas, lime circles straddling the plastic cups. It's a fairly slick operation. He sits in one of those folding lawn chairs that fit into a long sack like a rifle case, sipping on a cold one himself. Grinning like a leprechaun with his bag of coins on his washed-out plastic table, little FM radio on a string. It's way more than I can handle; I walk around the opposite way.

We meet at Joey's place, no reason except his basement is big enough. Joey lives on a quiet street and everybody likes it quiet, especially the newbies. Joey's is exactly two and a quarter miles from the nearest drink, Pokanos Bar and Grill. A little joint with dim lighting, stuffed deer heads on the walls, a big set of moose antlers. The bartender's a guy named Roger who sports a strawberry wraparound goatee and wears black T-shirts too small in the arms. I know the bus route to Pokanos off by heart. The others do too, whether they admit it or not.

I try to avoid the bus these days. And I don't drive either, though I still have my licence. My wife—my *ex-wife*—Crystal told me over and over not to drive under the influence. Not to drive in an altered state of mind. "Sooner or later, Lewis," she said. "Sooner. Or. Later."

But that was a lifetime ago. As of noon today, I've been sober exactly one year and the group is hosting a party in honour of my not fucking it all up. We're a small group so besides Joey, who's been dry a decade, no-one's reached twelve months without a slip. And it's unfortunate but everybody, all of them, will be there today. It's going to be a real red letter bash, an AA barn-burner. Coffee and cigarettes in shaky hands. Iced tea and juice. Cake with a big number twelve or *Way to Go!* on it. They'll slap me on the back, congratulate me. Firefly energy all over the room 'cause everyone associates a party with getting bombed. Someone's bound to sneak away early, catch the express bus to Pokanos. It happens every time.

If a person could go back in time, could he change the outcome of events? Or is everything set in motion and we just bounce around inside some giant, cosmic Mason jar, our lives determined by the guy who pokes holes in the lid for air? I often think about this on the walk to Joey's. It's my usual pre-meeting meditation and today, because it's an anniversary of sorts, I'm thinking of it more.

We've all discussed our pasts at the sessions. Memories of basement keg-nights, funnel parties, washroom-floor mornings with bathmat fibres stamped on our cheeks like worm tunnels. Phil, the Group Service Rep, told us once when he was fourteen he downed a two-six of Crown Royal swiped from his dad's liquor cabinet. Phil got so messed up he put his sister's dachshund in the microwave just like that urban legend or who knows, maybe Phil started the damn thing. He ran around the kitchen swatting his sister with a bag of buns yelling, "Hot dogs! Who wants hot dogs?" Later, unable to register what he had done, Phil told his sister, "I only had it on defrost." His face folded in on itself when he told us that story, his milk thistle eyebrows dragging his forehead down like rakes. Hard to imagine Phil was ever fourteen.

And then there's me, telling the story of how Crystal and I met. It was Halloween, Scare-aoke night at The Cranberry Arms. Crystal dressed up as Cleopatra and sang *Killer Queen*. But not me, I was too busy getting sozzled. Back then, my drinking had a certain charm, a mischievous quality like a young Dean Martin. Crystal doesn't know this but after I dropped her off I passed out behind the wheel of my tangerine Sunfire. Puked all over myself. Couldn't get the smell out of the car for weeks and had to fork out $50 for the rented Robin Hood costume.

We were married eight years, Crystal and I. How she managed to last that long I'll never know. When we had our daughter, Kimberly, I thought things might be different and I did stop drinking for a while. I couldn't enjoy a beer anymore with Kimberly's amethyst eyes staring. Her little harmonica cries as she searched for Crystal's breast, fingers grasping the air. So damned thirsty.

Joey keeps the lights low to match the mood. Today there are candles and a potluck finger-food brunch. It's supposed to be a party but everyone looks like they just buried a pet. I look around to see if I can guess who's going to bolt for Pokanos. Everyone here's a candidate.

Joey's trying hard to make this party work though, I'll give him that. There's a seven layer dip and a bowl of fruit punch, virgin-style. He's got the music going: Van Morrison, Melissa Etheridge, The Eagles, some techno band. Someone brought a tray of hotdogs and I just know it wasn't Phil. He's eyeballing those dogs like they're gonna spark to life. Keeps checking his watch, tapping his fingers on the frame of the Papasan chair he's gnarled into.

There are three rookies here today as well, each with less than six weeks under their belt. Marvin, Liza, and Raphael. Liza's husband brought her in the first time. She's teetering, an unlit Roman candle in a match factory. Raphael looks the same and Marvin I know has seen his share of ghosts. All three pigeons are hunkered by themselves. Nervous and jumpy as hot oil. Someone's gonna run, I can just smell it. The water-wagon's tilted and covered in grease, a cinch to fall off. Even easier with a tiny, vindictive push, if things were to suddenly go awry.

Step-programs are a joke, a gag everyone has heard. Still, we're basing our recovery on these twelve pop culture one-liners. Most of the steps are as substantive as swallowing wind, but it gets real at number eight—make a list of the people you screwed over. The big trip down blackout lane. Currently, I'm pinballing between steps nine and twelve: making amends to the people on my list and spreading the message. It's not a linear thing, you bounce around a lot. Like sidewalk hopscotch, a game of recovery leapfrog for addicts. One, two, three, Jump! *Jump!*

Crystal would've appreciated the patience in a thing like this. She kept hoping things would get better between us. Kept waiting for me to do the right thing, waiting for the real Lewis to emerge. Like watching a wriggly, grub-coloured cocoon, expecting butterflies to burst forth any second. That was one of the things I loved about Crystal, her nearly endless optimism.

I'm trying to write her a letter but how do you start something like that?

Hi Crystal, I know it's been a while, but I'm in this program, see? And I'm stuck on step nine....

Truthfully, I haven't seen Crystal since Kimberly's funeral. We never talked at the church, of course. Or at the cemetery. In fact, we haven't spoken a single word to each other since that day.

They tell us grief has a step program of its own, each stage as intense as a roomful of parrots. And anger. Jesus, anger's the strongest of all. This isn't the anger you feel when someone steals your parking spot at the mall. This anger compels you, owns you. Gives you the authority to do anything you can to ease the pain. The authority, even, to take someone's life if vengeance should overcome you.

Here in Joey's basement, everyone wears their anger like a badge pinned to their skin. I've heard all their clenched-teeth routines: Hello, my name is Raphael and I'm an alcoholic. I set fire to my trailer, watched the aluminum siding hiss while I sang *Tim Finnegan's Wake*. Hello, my name is Liza. I sold my wedding ring for vodka martinis. My name is Phil and I put a dog in a microwave oven, (but only on defrost). Hello, I'm Lewis and I killed my daughter in a car accident, watched her die in my arms. I saw her muscles twitch even after her brain went out. But get this folks, here's the kicker: I was stone cold sober at the time.

Kimberly used to put a blanket over me when I'd pass out. She'd leave a glass of water on the table and wait until I woke to see if we could go to the park. She loved that park—the swings, the dog run, the slide shaped like a corkscrew. Couldn't get enough of it. That's the thing about kids, they don't hold grudges. They don't condemn you. They just squeeze everything they can out of each moment, cover it over with sweet, powdery sugar.

A week before Crystal left, I found myself sprawled out on the living-room floor with one of Kimberly's blankets wrapped around me. I got up and searched for a drink, an eye-opener, hair of the dying dog. There wasn't a drop in the house.

I looked out the window. Kimberly had set up a table and chair outside on the sidewalk. I could see the back of her head as she handed out cups of lemonade, green Kool Aid, Fresca. There was a box of saltines on the table as well. Smart kid, I thought. Get them eating crackers then they'll be begging you for a cold drink. She was only six but sharp as cut glass.

It took me an hour to scrounge up enough money for a bottle. I put on a clean shirt and went outside. Kimberly was there at her stand. Little wet circles on the table-top. Sign taped to the edge that read, *Lemonade Free*.

She poured a glass. "For you, Daddy," she said. Look-what-I-can-do written all over her face.

"Free?" I said, looking at the sign. "Sweetie, what's all this?" I still had the booze money curled up in my fist, tight as a sac of spiders. "We can't just, you know, *give* stuff away. We don't have money to waste."

Kimberly just sat there.

"Do you know what waste is?" I said. She stared at me, my shirt half tucked, hair all messed. I poured the lemonade she gave me on the ground in front of the table. "See? That's a

71

waste." I dropped a stack of Premium Plus beside the spill, brought my runner down. Twisted my foot like a dancer.

I could feel the shakes coming on. My mouth was dry as a vacuum bag. I had to get a drink. I couldn't stand there any longer with Kimberly looking at me that way. "Just charge something, okay?" I told her as I trotted off to the liquor store, cracker crumbs stuck to the sides of my shoe.

"Here's to Lewis!" Joey says. "A role model of perseverance."

There's a dry spit of applause and a few soft-drink glasses are raised. Most of the group look away though and think about themselves, which is understandable. Marvin, especially, doesn't look my way. His eyes are closed and he's rubbing his temples like he's trying to read the future. He's jonesing something awful and he deserves every gut-twisting rip of it. The all-powerful, unquenchable ache.

I nod to everyone in the room and take a bite of a tuna fish Triscuit; it sticks in my throat like a tumbleweed. I don't think the newer members admire me as much as fear I'll look down on them now. As if I've suddenly become absolved of all my failures. The veterans know better, a year counts for less than a petrified turd.

I stopped drinking once before on my own, not long after Crystal left. Not a sip for a whole month. At the time, I thought Crystal and I might get back together and I couldn't wait to tell her how good it felt. Food tasted better, even the air smelled different. It was like surfacing after spending a year underground and someone hands you a bouquet of lilacs, some good tobacco, a bowl of cut oranges.

"I want to come back home," I told her when I picked Kimberly up. She stood there in the doorway, her hair tied back with an elastic, wearing an oversized ivory sweater.

It all seemed so perfect.

Then Crystal looked down at her feet. "I'm sorry Lewis," she said. "Kimberly and I, we're moving to Richmond. There's an opportunity there...but you can still see her.

Weekends, in the summer too. I'm sorry."

When I left Crystal's house with Kimberly beside me, I know my mind wasn't right. I was sober, but I wasn't thinking straight. Would it have made a difference if I'd been clear-headed? Would anything have made a difference? It wouldn't have altered the path of the other driver. Or the position of the Cocker Spaniel we both swerved to miss. It wouldn't have changed the location of the light pole, the shattered glass that burrowed into Kimberly and I like ticks. It's crazy, but I wonder if I had been drinking that night—just a couple shots—would I have reacted differently?

I blamed the man in the Tercel, the one that struck us, knocked us off the road. It was easier than blaming my own lack of attention. Easier than blaming the dog that ran in front of us, easier than blaming God. This man became the scapegoat. The centrepiece. The focus for all my vengeance.

Five months after the accident, I bought a couple bottles of Kressman white, alky screw-top wine. I went over to this man's house with the booze and some rocks I'd collected while scrounging for cans. The rocks were ideal for smashing things, palm-of-your-hand size and smooth as gunmetal. I hid in the junipers with the wine bottles on my lap, rocks in a pile beside me. All lit up like homemade fireworks with a lopsided grin and deep, flickering eyes. Anger makes you shine like that, makes you feel sober.

I sat under the bastard's window, rearranging the stones, numbering them with the sweat from my forehead, cradling them like penguin eggs. Waiting for him to appear. I threw the first stone, just to get his attention. It smashed through the middle of the glass, dark cracks zigzagging away like tad-poles. He came to the window after that and stared blankly through the hole. Stared right at me hiding in the bushes. His face a perfect, guilty target. I picked up stone number two and cocked my arm way back. As slow and steady and spiteful as the hand of God himself.

73

Sitting here in Joey's basement, I make the decision to leave out the twelve months of sobriety in my letter to Crystal. I don't want her to get the wrong idea and think I'm trying to reconnect. It has to be something simple.

Dear Crystal. There's no way to make amends for what I've done so I'm not even going to try.

Something like that.

Crystal did move to Richmond after the funeral like she'd planned, except without Kimberly of course. I know now that move was inevitable. Even if I'd been sober for a whole year instead of a month, she'd have done the same thing. If I could go back in time I wouldn't be able to stop her from going. I wouldn't even try.

If there was something I could change though, I'd go back and tell Kimberly it's okay to give out free lemonade and crackers. Then I'd sit there, far enough back so as not to interfere, and watch her work her magic.

Phil's wife baked the cake for the party. *Lewis* written in purple and blue, each letter struggling up a staircase of sticky white icing. Cute.

Marvin the newbie's in the corner holding a cup of coffee. His hands are rickety and he's watching the door like a fox. I know he's thinking about it, thinking about the two and a quarter miles to Pokanos Bar and Grill. Thinking about sipping highballs under the benedictory grins of deer and moose. I catch his gaze but he turns away and stares at the paper streamers. He never looks me right in the eye. Not ever. It's wrong I know, but I'm glad he's hurting.

You see Marvin was driving the other car the night Kimberly died. It was his face I zeroed in on with the rock. And I'm sure I would have nailed him too if I'd thrown that second stone. But just before I launched it, he collapsed and fell to the floor. Completely out of sight.

At the time I thought maybe someone unscrewed the lid to the cosmic jar and knocked Marvin of the way with

His finger. I dropped the stones and ran, tripping, drunk-stumbling, but never looking back. Wasn't long after that I joined the idiots here, became one of the AA alumni. It's a story so pathetic it makes me laugh every time. The story of the loser saved by God's greasy finger. The mason jar of forgiveness. The miracle of...what?

The tangible cause was much simpler. Marvin was drunk that night, drunker than I was. He passed out in front of the window in what can only be described as pisstank-perfect timing. I figured it out later when I dragged myself to Marvin's place to apologize, to offer money for the shattered window. No-one answered so I pushed on the unbolted door and found Marvin on the floor, naked and unconscious. There was an empty bottle beside him and his legs were folded in like a toothpick umbrella. Wax paper spread out on the ground to catch the puke. Pretty inventive. I knew from experience, a bowl can be hard to hit.

Today is Marvin's fourth meeting. He surprised the hell out of me when he first showed up. Like a sucker punch, below the belt, gloves off. Even now, I can't believe he's here. Of all the gin joints in all the towns in all the world....

There he goes. Marvin, sliding along the wall of Joey's basement like a ghost, heading for the door. Sweat beads rolling down his face like ant eggs. I knew he'd be the one to crumble.

Joey brings in some fresh coffee and Phil tunes the TV to a ball game. Then Liza starts breaking down in the corner and everyone focuses on that. No-one even notices Marvin slipping away but me. Try as I might, I can't ignore the opportunity. I follow him outside.

Even though the sun's beating down there are ice-chips under my skin and my whole body is numb. Marvin's at the bus stop. Hands in his pockets, knocking his head against the shelter, oblivious. When the bus shows up he almost breaks down the door to get in, exact change burning a hole in his hand. He sits in the very back seat, right by the rear doors. Leans his head down between his knees. I creep in after him and scrunch into a seat at the front, across from the driver. Marvin doesn't notice me. He's in his own world.

The drive only takes five minutes but the familiarity of the route makes it slow as hell. Marvin sparks to life as soon as we reach Pokanos. He jumps from his seat and slips out the rear of the bus. I get up from my hiding spot and watch him jog over to the building. He pauses at the door, rubs his hands through his hair, and then pushes through.

"Your stop?" the driver says to me as I stand there. I feel his eyes on the back of my head like a scalpel. I feel everyone's eyes.

"My stop," I say.

Roger's there in his usual position. He's shaved his goatee but otherwise nothing's changed. The bar still smells like a favourite chair; the air is still blue; the dead animals are still pinned to the walls, stiff and sombre as a jury. Roger nods to me mechanically and pours a shot of Jim Beam for Marvin, sets it down in front of him at the bar. Funny, I never figured him a bourbon man. I don't really know what kind of boozer he is but I do know one thing—he was as sober as I was that night in his Tercel. The police tested us both.

The irony of that still makes me angry. Angry mostly, at God. I see Him as a child picking up the Mason jar, holding it close to His pudgy face, giving it a wild shake. Watching worlds fall apart, over and over and over.

I walk up to the counter beside Marvin, put my hand on his drink. In one motion I pull it away and place it in front of me. The waves of alcohol quiver up from the glass, slide around us like baby snakes.

Marvin looks at me, stunned. "Oh Lewis. I'm, I'm..." he says. He starts to cry, smacks his palm against his forehead hard enough to stun a trout. He doesn't look like a killer to me. Doesn't look like part of a master plan either. I begin to

76

wonder if God didn't shake the jar after all. Maybe jars shake on their own, and for no good reason. Maybe that's just how it is.

I look Marvin in the eye. He's right there on the edge with me, gazing down into the pit. I lift the shot and do a mock cheers. Then I swirl the drink under my nose just like in the old days. My mouth opens, automatically, and I move the glass into position. The point of no return.

When the liquid touches my lips, I pause. Everything—the air, the stools, Marvin, the drink—seems suspended in mid-air like we're at the crest of a trampoline jump. I'm willing to wait like this for a second or two. Just long enough to see if Marvin will make a move. To see where the two of us might settle in the shaking jar.

JILL SEXSMITH

The Problem with Babies

You watch for Ava through the crack in your office door. She is coming to the gallery today to show off her newborn—something you both swore you would never do. You told her you refused to congratulate people for having sex without using birth control.

You have always thought of babies as being a bit like cancer—tumours with arms and legs. You have never understood why someone would willingly grow one. Your favourite word is barren. Your motto is *save yourself*. When invited to a baby shower, you always send a Diaper Genie and your regrets.

Recently though you've been feeling a bit restless, gassy, empty. You ask your doctor what all the rumbling is about; wonder if it's *the urge* you hear women talk about. You ask if having something tethered to your bellybutton, filling up your insides might be the cure.

"Don't get too crazy," he says, "it could just be an irritable bowel."

He recommends you snack on fennel seeds and sip ginger tea. So you do. You snack. You sip. Things seem to settle down.

When Ava arrives, the newborn is cradled in her arms—a tiny wailing thing wrapped in a blanket covered with ducks. She takes it to the lounge for its installation. She is pretty much your last friend to become a mother and, as these things go, the latest friend you have lost or are about to lose. You get out of your chair. You want to get your *ooh ah* over and done with. You want to get on with your day.

Ava and her baby quickly draw a group of admirers. You hide behind them and assess everyone's sincerity, willingness to lie, desperation to get out of work. Faces are scrunched up, lips are puckered, there are genuine sounding *oohs* and *ahs*, soft tickles on the baby's chin and cheeks.

"Awen't you pwecious."

You wonder what happens to Rs when a baby is present—an entire letter from the alphabet disappears.

Ava opens her diaper bag and the pristine lounge becomes a sprawling mess of gender-neutral toys and wet naps. You are used to an Ava carved by hard angles—tailored suits, nipped in at her tiny waist, hair cut blunt with a razor, stilettos worn like weapons. This Ava is soft around the edges, wears no make-up. This Ava has short hair and wears a leisure suit.

As a few people leave, you move closer. This Ava seems tired but happy. I am mother, hear me coo. When she sees you, she smiles a weary smile. You almost expect her to apologize for procreating. For being a traitor.

"Cute?" she says and points to her baby.

You shrug. During labour, this baby came out swinging and separated Ava's pelvis. You can't help but feel hostile toward something that has assaulted your friend and will never be formally charged. This is the problem with babies: no matter what they've done, parents tend to be proud of them. In most cases, they have only burst out of the womb causing great bodily harm. But what were they going to do? Stay in there?

When your co-worker is done goochy gooing the baby, she passes it off to you like a football. You wonder if it would be bad to drop a baby. Likely, perhaps, absolutely. If you do, no matter what you achieve in your career, you will always be known simply as The Baby Dropper. So you hang onto the baby while it cries and digs its nails into your forearms. When it opens its mouth, it reveals its flailing tongue. It has a wrinkly face and looks like an old man stuffed into a baby's body. You make the baby do a little air dance thing. You think it should probably skip college and fill out the pension application right away.

"Wee," you say, then set it on the table—very gently—propped up by books on Cubism and the Renaissance. The baby is scooped by someone else, which is when you notice its fingernails—impossibly tiny and delicate, attached to ten perfect little fingers.

"Do you have them manicured?" you ask.

Ava is busy wiping spittle and making a toy donkey bray but a co-worker tells you she used to bite her daughter's nails while she slept. You reach for the baby's hand and feel compelled to nibble. You have never considered fingernails before—these tender morsels.

"Are they a standard feature on all babies?" you ask.

Without really knowing who she is talking to, Ava says, "Yessy wessy they are. Yes, they are. Yes, they are."

You return to your office where you chew on a few fennel seeds. You remember asking Ava how she decided she wanted to have a baby. She told you she was watching figure skating on TV. One had nothing to do with the other. Not really. Except that now, whenever she thinks of her child, she also thinks of triple salchows and the one-foot lutz.

"But how did you know it was what you wanted?" you asked.

"My TV was on the fritz. It paused while Midori Ito was mid-leap. And I just said, by the time she lands, I want to have made a big decision. So I chose baby."

"Just like that?"

"Figure skaters," Ava said, "They fling themselves in the air and hope for the best. I wanted to do the same."

You spend the next hour tracing the little half-moon indents the baby left on your arm. When they fade completely, you are sad, lonesome, relieved to see them go.

After work, you drive to Itsy Bitsy—a baby clothing boutique. You owe Ava a gift and you want to shake off this fingernail business.

The boutique is sandwiched between your favourite shoe store and café. Women with babies always come in, charging toward the espresso machine with their strollers, expecting people to move for them like they've got some sort of disability. Or they take up three times the space they need—parking strollers, baby seats, and pop-up jumpy castles in the middle of the floor. The mothers look proud of their children as they entertain the crowd. You have always occupied one table, one chair. You pride yourself on being compact. You entertain no-one.

Inside Itsy Bitsy, the store clerks hover around a stroller. A baby's designer booties kick the air. The mother beams at the child like it's her project, her exhibition, just a small sample from her successful breeding program. As you get closer, the baby is gnawing on a rubber set of keys. It, too, has the teensy fingernails.

You look for an outfit for Ava's baby. Mother Ava who said she never wanted a baby and can't even make two-sided photocopies. You sift through the racks. The clothes are overpriced, ridiculous, slowly winning you over. You grab an outfit and admire, mock, covet it.

"That's a onesie," the clerk says.

You figure onesies are part of the problem not part of the solution but you say you'll take it and a few other things you've grabbed.

"When are you due?" The clerk starts rolling the onesie so it looks like a pansy.

You almost laugh then say, "May. Early May." You rub your stomach clockwise then counter.

"Congratulations," the clerk says, "wait right here."

She leaves then comes back holding a platter with a mini-bundt cake on it. The top is shaped like a pregnant woman's stomach. She sticks a sparkler in the belly button and lights it. The hissing makes others gather around. They sing a congratulations jingle.

You sign up for Itsy Bitsy e-news. The Itsy Bitsy team is part of your family now, here to help you through this. You promise to let them know the very second you give birth. You start to think about the advantages of being pregnant: pre-boarding, the best parking spots, being congratulated for doing nothing, fucking, the miracle of life. When you are an expecting mother, no-one cares that you can't tie your own shoes. They don't stop you on the street and ask to see your CV. People just want to rub your tummy, buy you things, feed you.

You stand with your Itsy Bitsy sisters until the sparkler blows itself out. Motherhood already makes you feel a bit guilty.

After work, you drive to your husband's office. He is still at work because he is too kind to say no to a patient mourning the death of one of seventeen cats. On the way to his office, you caress the baby clothes—a ruffled skirt, a sailor dress, frilly underwear. Pink Mittens. The teensiest mittens, likely knitted by an elf. You want to frame these mittens. You suppose unisex clothes would have been more practical but if you were going to have a baby, she would have to be a girl. She'd have no choice. You refuse to bake a penis. For a moment, you forget these clothes are supposed to be a gift for your friend.

At Eric's office, you walk in and say, "Our baby-making sex will be the best we've ever had."

"This is sudden." He taps his desk with a pencil, looks worried, amused, bored.

"Sometimes it works this way."

"Since this morning when I saw you take your birth control?"

"Things change in a split second. Between this morning and that moment, there were 10,000 seconds and that many chances to change."

"Do you remember when you demanded we get exchange students so you could practice your Mandarin? Or when you wanted to install a saltwater fish tank so you could quit your job and breed seahorses?"

You finger an Itsy Bitsy soother in the bottom of your purse and want to shove it in his mouth. Of course you remember these things. "All wonderful ideas," you say.

His assistant pages him. His next patient is here.

"Mrs. Jamison?" you ask. "Is she the one who pulls out her eyelashes?"

He nods. "You can't return a baby by the way. Even if you keep the receipt." He kisses your forehead, opens the door, and ushers you out.

"Our baby's name is Jade by the way. Thought you should know."

When you get home, you wander around. In your home gym, you sit on a balance ball. You turn on the treadmill and watch it spin.

In the bathroom, you grab your packages of birth control. You have never missed a day because there is no excuse for missing a day, unless you were dead or in a coma, in which case you wouldn't be having sex anyway. You lift the toilet lid, twirl the dial, and let the days fall.

When Eric comes home, you ask for an update on Mrs. Jamison's eyelashes.

"All accounted for."

"Phew."

He grabs your hand, which is how you know he is about to share a big thought, tell a joke, divorce you.

"I think right now, exchange students are a better idea for us. I'd even go for the seahorses or a couple of Chihuahuas. You could buy them matching coats."

"I can do the baby thing," you say, more or less to convince yourself.

When Eric goes to bed, you stay up and think about the social experiment you did in high school. Everyone was assigned a raw egg baby and was charged with taking care of it for a week. You went home and scrambled yours immediately. The next day, when you told your teacher you had eaten your baby, she started the Child and Family Services paperwork and you failed the unit.

85

With no eggs in the house to prove yourself, you get out a small bag of flour and put the Itsy Bitsy sailor dress and frilly underwear on it. You give the sack a happy, impartial, convincing face and glue on some wool for hair.

"I wuv you Gwacie Wacie."

For the next week, you take Grace with you. You shop and run errands on the other side of town. You pull a blanket over Grace's face, shush anyone who tries to talk to you, bare your teeth at anyone who tries to get near the stroller. With more persistent, nosey, bitchy, we're-all-in-this-together mothers, you talk quietly of colic, teething, the convenience of caesarean sections. Occasionally, you have to stick Grace in your purse or desk drawer.

At the end of the week, there is nothing left of Grace but an empty bag. You try again. Grace II. At the end of the week, there is about one cup of Grace left. You're getting the hang of it. You go through a few more Graces until you're ready to strike a deal. You bring Eric coffee in bed and introduce him to your love child, Grace. You do not mention the seven sisters that died before her.

"If I can keep her alive for seven days, you have to do me with baby making intentions. On demand."

He scratches Grace's chin and sips his coffee.

"Okay, but it looks like the baby already has a leak."

After one week of top-notch parenting, Grace has mostly retained her shape and you resubmit her, like a portfolio, for evaluation.

You stand back and watch while Eric inspects her, pausing on the glue and duct taped areas. He wipes his hands, *lightly* dusted with flour.

"I could have made three dozen muffins with this baby last week, now I could only make one."

Before he says anything else, you demonstrate how to change Grace's cloth diaper. You jiggle her up and down. You burp her.

"She still has a pulse. What more do you want?"

After work, Eric lies in bed waiting—the look on his face a mixture of hope and dread.

"I can't do it with the flour sack watching."

You turn Grace toward the wall.

"You know it's a myth that lying with your legs in the air will help you conceive?" Eric says.

You are negotiating with the baby gods. Convincing them you will fold yourself into whatever post-coital contortions you need to. If they could just send Jade down the pipeline. Pronto.

At work, you make final arrangements for an exhibition opening. You should be briefing yourself on the artist and history of his work. Instead, you read up on what to expect while you are pregnant—hormone fluctuations, morning sickness, frequent urination, an inner glow.

At the opening, you should mingle, this is your job. You do wonder more and more about the contributors and what makes them support art. Last month the gallery was filled with a bunch of bananas dangling from the ceiling. The artist measured each string and applied a particular knot to each stem. As they ripened, they were removed and made into banana bread. Proceeds from the resulting bake sale were donated to the local food bank.

This exhibition is a bunch of hay bales scattered around the gallery. Several walls had to be removed to accommodate the round ones. In your press release the artist wanted you to stress the importance of scent and placement. "My work is all about symmetry and the spaces in between," he said. "Also, if people want to take a piece of the hay to chew on, they can. These pieces are interactive."

You sip ginger ale and approach one of the guests. "Scent is so evocative, don't you think?" You sniff one of the bales.

"These bales are bullshit," she says, tips her head back, and empties her glass.

You are relieved and gesture for her to sit down. She does not want to talk bales. She eats her sushi with a knife and fork and tells you she had to put down her Ragdoll cat because she just bought a leather sofa—like this one—only white. She pets the sofa like it's a big friendly cow. While she tells you how much she liked her Ragdoll, the way he pawed her face in the morning and wanted kibble, all you can think about are nursery colours and peeing on plastic strips.

Tick tock. You have read that visualizing and convincing yourself you are actually pregnant will make it so. To really get into it, you call in morning sickness for the next few weeks.

"Congratulations. I didn't realize you were pregnant."

"It came on fast," you say.

Your director says you can work from home if you are up to it, give a shit, want to keep your job. He sends you photos of the next exhibition—a bunch of painted twigs. He includes notes from the artist who has elaborated on the exact position his twigs were in when he found them. Prone on a beach. Vertical in a rubbish bin. Lying in mourning on the sidewalk.

Although Eric objects, you hire a designer for the nursery. A designer who insists on painting in lemon, lime, and orange—a sherbet motif. You want to lick the walls every time you come in. When you told him you were having a girl, he insisted on adding his signature castle mural called lullaby princess.

After working with him for a month, he finally asks, "So honey, when are you due? You're flat as a board."

"I'm about three months along," you say, hoping he's working on the final strokes of the knight's jousting spear and you will never see him again.

Jade is coming—she is just fashionably late.

At the doctor's office, you shift in the hard plastic chair and read back issues of women's magazines. You learn all about having an addiction to teeth whitening, the 25-minute casserole, and last year's new fall colours. You have a male gynaecologist. You try to convince yourself you don't hate this but you do. You try to tell yourself he comes highly recommended but you don't care. When the nurse calls your name, your vagina knows instinctively to clench.

Your doctor is an efficient man who, you are convinced, snaps on those gloves before touching his wife too. As you put your legs in the stirrups, he tells you to scoot closer to the edge and makes hand gestures. "Scoot. Scoot. Scoot."

You inch your way down and do your best to think of last year's new fall colours.

When you get your baby-making diagnosis back, your doctor hands it over like a fish still flopping on a silver platter.

"Many things are working against you."

"Like?"

"You've got a hostile womb, your age, you have an acidic pH, and your uterus is tilted and shaped like a heart."

That doesn't sound so bad. Who wouldn't want to spend the first nine months of their life wrapped in a heart?

"See this?" He taps the backlit image and you know you are about to be taught a lesson. "See where the heart cleaves? Less room for a child to grow. It would likely pop out early."

When you get to your car, you search your handbag for the Itsy Bitsy bundt cake. It is still wrapped in its little stork-shaped box. The belly is stale and mostly crushed now but you moisten it with your fingertips and try to reshape it. When the little mound can't be put back together, you take a bite of what remains.

At home, you turn into a puddle in Eric's lap. He was such a good sport about masturbating into the cup and rushing it off for testing. You were 100% certain he was the problem.

He had stubborn sperm. Lazy sperm. Not enough sperm. New Age sperm that didn't like to compete. Something was wrong with the assembly line. They were all heads. Or tails.

He runs his fingers through your hair and as you explain your hostile womb, you feel like a woman with two hearts—neither works.

You call in miscarriage. You don't have a choice. You need to reset your babymeter back to zero months. You stay home for a week. When you return, everyone is extra nice but no-one says a thing.

You have always pitied couples who say, "not yet, but we're trying." So, you keep your efforts quiet but you do keep trying.

Then, at the one-year point, you stop. Order a cease and desist. Only there is nothing to stop except peeing on plastic strips and eating excessive amounts of folic acid. There is no point in taking birth control again since you can't get pregnant. There is no point in stopping sex, you're not an idiot. You just don't have to lie there with your legs in the air and pray to the baby gods. You can stop giving a shit about if and when your eggs have dropped. Basket's empty. You take your ovulation chart off the fridge. It likely wasn't the best foreplay. The only thing you really have to stop is thinking about her—imagining yourself as a mother. You figure you would have been a terrible one anyway. When you were a kid, your hamster did get lost in the wall.

You fill one of Jade's baby bottles with Chardonnay, go into the nursery, and turn off the lights. The mobile above her crib spins and five princesses mock you. You deserve to be mocked. With the stress of trying to conceive you have actually lost weight. You run your hand over your stomach. Your hip bones protrude. Your stomach is concave. You crawl into Jade's crib, suck her bottle, and fall asleep.

In the middle of the night, you wake and sit in the crib. Grace VIII is sitting on the change table. You grab her and take her into the garden where you dig a hole. You lay her in it and pull a blanket up to her chin. You want to sing a lullaby or a hymn, something comforting, distracting, mournful. All you can think of is the Itsy Bitsy jingle. "Everything's going to be okay Gwacie Wacie. Yes, it is. Yes, it is."

You slowly cover Grace with dirt and replant the wilting peony.

Inside, there is white flour everywhere but you leave it. It is so quiet in here. You wonder if it is newly quiet or if it has always been like this. You are determined to fill this house some other way. You consider fostering a child, becoming a block parent, studying to be a doula.

You research adoption online. There are crack babies, unwanted babies, babies of teen mothers, unwed mothers, terminally ill mothers. There are special needs babies and older children in foster care with profiles like: *Davey is a smiley, happy-go-lucky fellow. And handsome too! He is doing well in his special education classes but is still having a hard time with grief. Since he hit puberty, he often hits others and has a difficult time controlling his rage. He shows great imagination in the way he acts out. Davey has been in foster care since he was six. He needs a forever home. Adopt Davey today!*

Sorry Davey.

There are also foreign babies: Russian, Ukrainian, Chinese. You decide on twin girls from China and order them online. They will cost approximately $30,000 each. Estimated delivery time is three years.

You decide to drive to Eric's office to tell him about your children from Yangshuo. If he's not available, you'll talk to his assistant or one of the patients waiting in the lobby.

You think you've got problems?

You go out to your car and imagine securing your twins into their seats. Wonder where you can buy one of those bumper stickers: *Caution. Babies on Board!* As you pull out of your driveway, you sing the ABCs. You are prepping your children for preschool. You can never start too young, and these things get competitive.

While you drive, you see Liang and Mei growing up: teething, mashed food, whole food, diapers, potty training, first words, first steps, bedtime stories, training wheels, Band-Aids, school pictures, matching clothes, non-matching clothes, play dates, bunk beds, separate rooms, bunk beds, baton twirling, summer camp, soccer, horses, trombone and flute, duets, school plays, homework, art on the fridge, first crushes, inappropriate outfits, hidden piercings, insecurities, heartbreaks, the sex talk a little too late, all-girls school, plaid kilts and knee-highs, sneaking out at night, secret codes, cell-phone plans, high school graduation.

By the time you get to your turnoff, you are exhausted and the girls are in university—Yale and Harvard. Liang is finishing medicine and will work for Doctors Without Borders. Mei is studying mediation and will broker peace deals in the Congo. They are so modest. You know they didn't get this from you.

You can't change lanes so you take the next exit and circle back. There are signs for the airport and soon you are on your way to pick up your daughters. They came to you a year ago and told you they wanted to return to their homeland to explore their heritage before they started their careers.

They said they were hesitant to ask because they didn't want to offend you—because you had been such a wonderful mother. Because you had given them everything: a good life, ponies, haircuts they don't hate you for. They had been organically fed, drank filtered water, were immunized. They said they had to make this pilgrimage and they had to do it on their own. It was something they had to do for themselves. Although it wasn't how you had pictured things working out, you knew you had to find a way to live without them, find a way to move on. So you let them go. You sent them off. You wished them well and watched them leave you. You prayed they wouldn't look for their real mother. "She's just DNA!" you wanted to say. You thought about running out onto the tarmac and waving their plane back to the gate. But you let them take off. You let them fly away. You knew it was best for everyone.

You're good that way.

A Box Full of Wildebeest

I'm sitting in my apartment in Japan when mother calls to tell me she's had an abnormal Pap smear. I write down the words Pap smear and wonder how telephone lines work anyway? Are they like under the ocean? Is there a big whale swimming over our words? Pap smear. Pap smear. Pap smear.

When I don't respond, she says, "Maybe I should come for a visit?"

While mother talks about abnormal squamous cells lining up along her cervix like a firing squad, I tear one paper square out of my shoji screen and look through the hole. I had imagined a life here filled with strolls under cherry blossom trees with my geisha friends. I wanted to see hot tub monkeys hot tubbing in the wild. I wanted to hang out. Put my arm around a hairy shoulder. I was also supposed to befriend a Zen master, embrace Buddhism, levitate. While floating, I would tell other people they had it all wrong.

So far, my vision and reality haven't matched up.

"I might have radiation," my mother says. "Nuke my cervix."

I feel a small earthquake and listen to my dishes rattle. I listen for a tsunami warning and look out my window to see if anyone in my building is leaving for higher ground. All is quiet. No 40-metre waves in sight.

"Yes, now is a good time for a visit."

There is a temple in Kyoto. I can't remember the name and it doesn't matter because there are a million of them in that holy city that sells hand-painted scrolls alongside Hello Kitty telephones. The important thing to know is that there are thousands of teeny tiny steps going up and there are thousands of teenier tinier steps going down. It's as if people's feet are expected to shrink by the time they get to the top, as if the air at a higher altitude in Kyoto has feet-shrinking

94

properties.

Somehow, my mother and I with our big, North American feet, make it to the top. We rub a laughing Buddha belly, choke on incense and admire the view. Before we leave, we buy paper prayers and hang them on a string.

"What does it mean?" I ask a man in my shattered Japanese.

"No good," he says. He sucks wind and waves us away.

My mother undoes her prayer and stuffs it in her pocket. "This place is trying to curse me."

On the way down, I take the teenier tinier steps three, four at a time, daring this country to trip me. When I look back, my mother is navigating each stair slowly, carefully. Her big feet hang over the edge and threaten to topple her. Going sideways is no better; her feet seem as wide as they are long. For a moment, I mistake her expression as *I can do it myself* determination. But when I put on my sunglasses, I realize her look is more *afraid of a broken hip in a foreign country*.

"You remember Ken Wilson's daughter?" she asked me during the Pap smear conversation. "She's over there too. She got run over by a bus in South Korea. Her parents had to charter a plane to bring her home. Poor thing was screaming in agony because those people couldn't set a bone properly."

My mother has always admired Ken Wilson's daughter. Although we often did similar things, she did them for better reasons. I was in Japan looking for a kimono and a hot tub monkey while she was in Seoul working in an orphanage. In my mother's head, if I were Ken Wilson's daughter, I would take her hand, slowly guide her down the steps and warn her about the perils of the Asian healthcare system. Instead, I slowly move toward her and know that even if I get there, I'll never quite make it.

I'm sitting in my apartment in Paris when a carrier pigeon lands at my window. I take the note attached to its leg.

I have lumps on my ovaries. Maybe now is a good time for a visit?

95

When my mother arrives, we carry her kiwi-sized tumours up the Eiffel Tower, stroll with them along the Seine.

"Smells like piss," one tumour says.

It does smell like a urinal so we go back to street level and rest with them for a while in Notre Dame. We rent bikes, put the tumours in the baskets along with our baguette, and go looking for the tunnel Princess Diana died in.

"So sad," my mother says and extends her hand to the ghost of a princess.

"We look like tourists," one of the tumours says.

I suggest we spend the rest of the day at a museum.

"Fine. Have it your way," my mother says.

In front of the Mona Lisa, the tumours get lumpier and harder to hold.

"All this way just to see an ugly lady smirk?" one tumour says.

When the tumours get squirmy and grow sick of looking at art in the Louvre, my mother says "Fine!" Then she packs them into her suitcase along with her French linens and carries them back across the Atlantic, business class.

I'm walking along Bondi Beach when I come across a conch. I put it to my ear and hear my mother calling out over the sound of the ocean waves. "I only have one ovary left. I better get my good one to Australia, immediately."

When she arrives, we placate the good ovary. We carry it between us to the opera house. We buy it its own seat.

"I never liked Verdi," the ovary says at intermission. It complains about the crowd and the perfumed women.

The next day, we swim with it in the ocean. I take it surfing. We catch a wave. We all get massages on the beach. Later, we walk it across the harbour bridge and stop halfway. Despite our pampering, the ovary has become slippery and heavy, says it misses its sister. It is supposed to be healthy but has started to sprout hair and teeth. The ovary starts to snap and grabs hold of my mother's finger.

96

"Everything turns on me," my mother says.

On the count of three, we throw it in the water and watch it float. It hangs on the surface then disappears. When it finally sinks, she grips the rail for a moment. Then she reaches into her purse and pulls out a calculator and an envelope with all of her receipts in it. She starts adding things up, then says, "With all the money I've spent coming to visit you, I could have built a sunroom."

I'm huddled around my radiator in Moscow when it starts tapping out Morse code. It is mother telling me her liver is failing.

"You won't like the language here," I tap back.

"Why not?"

"They speak machine gun."

"But I've already booked my ticket."

"The people here are sad and grey. It will upset you."

"But so much history," she taps.

"And yet, they could only come up with two names for an entire population. Natasha and Alexander."

"Don't forget Nikita and Vladimir."

I meet my mother at the airport with a metal tray. She slaps her liver on it and we walk into the winter night. Her mood is lighter. She seems rosy in the cold wind; a wind that only tries to steal things from me, blow soup from my spoon, swipe at my pockets, lift up my skirt. Large Soviet snowflakes fall as we walk through Red Square—our heads and shoulders conquered. My mother holds the tray out as if she's walking through a cafeteria. The liver wobbles like Jell-O. An old man sits hunched on the steps of Saint Basil's Cathedral and asks, "Can I buy that?"

"This is so Tolstoy," she says and keeps walking. Communism agrees with her.

Outside the Kremlin seems like a strange place to talk about summer camp. "Remember how happy you were?" she says.

"Actually, I hated having to swing on a rope across that ditch. I prayed I'd fall and break my arm so I could go home. I hated making picture frames with macaroni. I hated making those stupid edible necklaces. I hated the buddy system, because I hated my buddy."

"I see," she says. "That camp was expensive. It was a privilege to attend." She stops to watch a Russian couple talking. All conversations here sound like arguments. "I remember that frame. You never put my picture in it."

"It was a gift. You were supposed to put a picture in it."

"I'm not sure why you insisted I come on this trip if you're only going to tell lies." She disappears into the snowy night and takes her liver with her.

In a sleeper car on the Trans-Siberian someone knocks on my door. When I open it the attendant smiles and puts a banana to her ear. I follow her to another compartment. She points to the phone then turns her back as if I'm about to get undressed.

"What if I were dying? What if I were really dying?" my mother asks.

"Are you?" The train rumbles beneath my feet and I brace myself.

"I could be."

"Well, if you were really dying, I'd come home and take care of you."

"I'm going to die alone in a ditch somewhere. I just know it."

"Are you dying?" The wind howls through windows that never seem to close properly.

"I just have eczema right now but it's very itchy. Should I meet you?"

"It's very cold in Siberia. It will only make your skin worse."

When I get off the train in Omsk, my mother is standing there in short sleeves, arms outstretched. I'm not sure if it is an invitation to embrace or if she just wants to show me her rash.

"Didn't you bring a proper jacket?" I ask.

"Are you concerned? Are you showing concern for me?"

"Did you come to Siberia without a winter jacket?"

"I wanted to feel what Dostoyevsky felt."

"You won't be doing hard labour in a gulag. Have you even read Dostoyevsky?"

"No, but I have a collector's copy of The Brothers Karamazov."

My mother is shaking so I give her my coat and we go looking for proper clothes. I try to use her for a windbreak but she says, "It's your trip. You lead the way. Just pretend like I'm not here."

By dim street light, we move toward the shops. There is an eerie beauty here, sad snow that makes a peculiar moaning sound as we walk. The city's streets are unusually wide. Wind gathers speed and goes unchecked. There are rules and no rules. We are blown along. All of the buildings here are over-sized to make people feel small and nervous. Every one of them feels full of secrets. Ever since I arrived in this country, I have felt imaginary crosshairs trained on me. As if some KGB spy on a rooftop was going to take me out.

"Honestly, you're so paranoid," my mother says.

At the clothing store we both buy Russian hats and sable fun-fur coats. My own jacket doesn't stand up to Siberia cold. Without looking at me, the storekeeper inspects my roubles with a magnifying glass. When she turns away, I take the coats and hats and quickly walk out.

"Now what?" my mother asks.

We take shelter in a doorway. I grab my map titled *Bird's Eye View of Omsk (pictures made from a plane)* and we march around the city in our matching hats and coats. I read my brochures as we go. "In spring and summer city is filled with beautiful gardens and flovers."

"Flovers," my mother says. "I guess they'd be frozen flovers now."

"Yes, I guess they would." I pull my hat down and brace against a wind so cold it splits my bones.

In the hotel, we sit on our beds and stare at each other, cold and exhausted, still wearing our hats and coats. "How do people live here?" I ask.

"You're omsking the wrong person."

I smile and would love to give that a pity laugh but I'm not that generous.

My mother takes off her hat. "I wish I had been funnier."

We eat dinner at the hotel where we are promised, "The aroma alone will dragged you in." The cutlery is heavy and takes two hands to lift. The plates are edged with gold but only the stubborn bits remain. Through the window, I watch two soldiers walk side by side through the snow, heading toward a birch forest. I look again and they are single file. They stop to drink from a flask and have a laugh. White clouds puff out their noses and mouths. The younger one is laughing so hard, he falls to his knees and holds his sides. The other points his gun at the fallen one's head. Then he reaches out to help him up. When I look again, they're gone.

After dinner, my mother and I go back to our room. Silent. There is only so much to say about crumbling organs and cracking flesh. My mother strips and can't stop rubbing her arms and back on the red velvet curtains. I pull the ear flaps on my hat down to block out the shush-shushing and fall asleep.

In the morning, I see she spent the night making a ball gown out of the curtains. It actually looks nice—very Russian, but nice.

"This feels so good against my skin."

On our way to the station, my mother—in her hat, sable fun-fur and red velvet curtain—stops to look at her reflection. "Funny," she says and twirls.

We both start to laugh. We get on the train and don't get off until Vladivostok.

In India, I live in a hut with a thatched roof and mud floor. One of the boys from the village brings me a tin can attached to a string. "Hello," I say.

"My mammogram shows I have a lump. Maybe now is a good time for a visit?"

"I have Giardia. I'm not feeling well myself."

"Well, it's not cancer. I'll bring you some Pepto-Bismol."

It takes hours to get from the airport to my hut outside of Mumbai but my mother, champion sufferer, says nothing as we inch our way forward. Beside a crowded market we have to wait two hours for an elephant to finish taking a nap. While we wait, people try to sell us gold bangles, hoop earrings, beautiful saris and shawls. Small children crowd our tuk-tuk and ask us for pens. The driver ignores us except when the elephant finally gets up and sways its penis back and forth.

"American women," he says, "this will be a good photo to capture with your camera."

My mother has the defective boob in a basket, covered with a cloth like a warm loaf of bread. To let it see, she takes the cloth away.

"Hi boob," I say.

The boob sits in its basket, surveying the situation. It jiggles a bit. The boob doesn't like India at all.

"Remember that time when Rachel Sanders punched you in the stomach and I had to go to her parents' house and I had that big fight with her mother?" she asks.

I open a new package of pens. "I don't remember that at all. I remember you saying if I was kinder, I wouldn't get punched in the stomach by nice little girls."

"Honestly, you have such an imagination."

Indian children are always smiling. "And, I remember you became friends with Rachel's mother shortly after that."

"No, that was much, much later."

"No, it wasn't."

"What are you saying?"

I want these children to tell me how a pen can make them

so happy. A pen! "I'm saying you practically congratulated, no, you practically adopted Rachel Sanders after she punched me in the stomach."

"Why must you ruin our vacations like this? Rachel was a nice girl." My mom covers up the boob. "You don't have to listen to this."

The boob doesn't like the pollution in Mumbai, or Agra, refuses to smile for photos at the Taj. I offer it curry, fresh flowers from the market, a job in a call centre, but it refuses. The boob perks up a little in Varanasi so we sit with it on the banks of the Ganges where bodies wrapped in colourful silks surround us.

My mother whispers to the boob for a long time. It's hard to say goodbye to a boob. "Did you know you always preferred to suck from this boob when you were a baby?"

"I thought it looked familiar."

My mother walks into the river and dunks the boob. She washes it gently as bodies float by. All around me, fires burn. The strange outlines collapse and cave in on themselves in ways bodies shouldn't. I see my mother press the boob to her chest. She puts the boob back in the basket and walks to the shore. We gather sticks and build a raft for the boob. We place it in the centre and bind it in place with red silk. We both walk into the Ganges and watch it float alongside, then overtake a corpse.

"It was always a competitive boob," my mother says.

On the Serengeti, elephants rumble past my tent. The woman I'm sharing this tiny space with is a photographer. She calmly looks at images on her camera and tells me that elephant tears are the same chemical composition as ours.

"Why don't they step on us?" I ask.

"I think it's because they know how that would feel."

Over her shoulder, I watch as she flips past images of the lone Syringa tree at twilight, the elusive leopard, a giraffe and its baby reaching for the same branch. When the elephants are gone, our guide comes to our tent and hands me his walkie-talkie. I hear my mother's voice.

"Breaker breaker. I've got carpel tunnel. Maybe now is a good time for a visit? Back over."

"Ten-four. What's your twenty?"

"I'm travelling with a herd of wildebeest. Do you copy?"

"Copy that. When will you be here?"

"10-43 at the watering hole. Something about a hungry alligator."

"Roger. See you in the morning."

"Ten-four that."

"Who was that?" the photographer asks.

"My mother. She's on her way to meet me."

"That sounds really nice. I wish my mother loved me that much." She goes back to flipping through her images.

In the morning, our guide tells me he can't hold up the tour for my mother, who will be joining us as soon as the herd of wildebeest arrives.

"We've got gorillas to see. It's misty, the conditions are perfect," he says.

"It sounds far-fetched, but she will be here."

"I'm sorry. We can't wait."

As our jeep convoy starts out, I hear the rumbling of a thousand hooves moving across the plains. Through a cloud of dust, I see my mother riding one of the wildebeest, her single boob bouncing for all it's worth.

As they approach our convoy, her wildebeest stops and kneels down to let her off. She waves goodbye to it with the hand in its little carpel tunnel brace, and the beast canters off. "You didn't have to wait for me," she says as she squishes into our jeep.

"Do you have any luggage?" I ask.

"I was travelling by wildebeest. There are weight restrictions."

Our guide stares at my mother through the rear-view mirror and almost crashes into a tree.

"I had to leave all liquids behind. Can I have a sip?" she asks the photographer and reaches for her canteen.

"Have as much as you want." The photographer starts taking photos of my mother with more enthusiasm than a feasting lion.

"Here," my mother gives me the canteen. "Open this. Can't you see I've got carpal tunnel?"

She tries to look natural for the photographer but can't resist posing for a few. When the photographer turns her attention to a lost baby zebra, my mother says, "There, now you'll have something spectacular to put in that macaroni frame."

In Beijing, I'm walking past a cellphone kiosk when the salesman runs after me, taps me on the shoulder and passes me a phone. "It's for you," he says.

I shrug my shoulders and put the phone to my ear.

"Kidney failure," she says. "Maybe now is a good time for a visit?"

Beside me, a man horks into a spittoon.

"I can hear you nodding," my mother says. "See you soon."

As we walk along the Great Wall, it's hard moving from station to station. The stairs are steep and crumbling, big stones slip out from under our feet, German elbows dig into our ribs. The kidney is bitchy and complains about the heat and crowds. It asks my mother to stop drinking water.

"It's very unappreciative," my mother says, looking directly at me.

We keep climbing. I try my best to slow down, to offer my arm for support, but I'm falling too. The farther we go, the more yellow my mother becomes. Not yellow-yellow, like sun yellow, but mustard yellow with grey undertones, maybe a hint of olive green. She is the shade of yellow no-one's mother should ever be.

"I think we should go back now," I say.

"For what? I can be seen from space right now."

"That's a myth. I think you need help."

"Oh, and you're going to help me?"

I watch the step she is on wobble back and forth. "Yes, I'm going to help you." I'm going to give her one of my own kidneys—a replacement part.

I hire a mule and we ride into the village. I draw pictures for the doctor and we are given a mixture of what tastes like red wine and hemp seed. I fall asleep looking at jars filled with turtle shells, dried snakes, strange fruits and long branches.

"Good luck," the doctor says in perfect English.

As my mother starts to go under, she tells me she wishes I had been a doctor or a lawyer. Somebody. "What are you anyway?" she asks. "What am I supposed to tell people you *do*?"

"Tell them I'm a runner."

The next time I wake, I know there will be less of me.

After the transplant, we are moved to a real hospital in the city where we recover side by side.

"This is my daughter," my mother tells the doctor, the nurse, the orderly, the janitor, the other patients in the room. "She saved my life. Isn't that the most amazing thing you've ever heard?"

They all nod politely then move on to their next mess. We both keep lifting up the bandages to look at our stitches.

I'm sitting in my old room, in the house I grew up in, when mother calls me downstairs.

"How does That Nurse expect me to eat pizza when I can't swallow properly?"

Her nurse shrugs, points to the can of Ensure and continues changing the bed sheets. "It's liquid. Only sip what you feel like."

"Bullshit," my mother says. "Now there's a pepperoni

stuck in my throat." She leans forward, parts her gown and waves me over. "Here, rub my back but don't use your nails." The nurse holds the gown open while I work over my mother's back in gentle circles. "That's so nice, dear. That Nurse doesn't know what she's doing."

Although it is at someone else's expense, I cannot remember the last time she complimented me. Years ago, she told me I had nice eyebrows (this was after I had plucked them into a thin line). She also told me I had nice knees, "Normally the ugliest part of a woman's body." And, now, apparently I can rub a back.

"I can't breathe." My mother's voice is raspy. "That Nurse keeps waterboarding me."

The nurse slips an oxygen tube over my mother's head and into her nose. I listen to the soft hiss of air.

"I want to be cremated." My mother squeezes my hand. "And I want you to spread me into the water while standing on that bridge in Australia where we had such a nice time. And don't take the lid off the container and just dump me in a big clump. I want to fan out into the water in a graceful arc."

I squeeze her hand. My mother closes her eyes and leans back. As she rests, I say, "It's okay. I'm here. Just like I told you I would be."

She sits up. "You're only here because you ran out of continents."

"There's still Antarctica."

"Just go," she says. "Play with the penguins. I always knew I'd be alone."

I rub my transplant scar. "I'm not sure what you want?"

"Get the hair out of your eyes. There's a pretty girl hiding in there somewhere. A skinny one too." She coughs and rests her head on her pillow.

"I'm leaving," I say.

"Surprise, surprise," she says.

As I go upstairs, my mother tells her nurse, "My daughter

gave me one of her kidneys but kept the good one for herself."

I'm walking through my old house—empty now yet somehow filled with her. In my room, under the bed, there is a box marked *miscellaneous failures*. Inside is evidence of my flunked childhood: the macaroni frame with no picture; my report cards, with low grades highlighted; my letters from camp, with grammar and spelling notations in the margins. Everything is carefully dated and filed. She has been the curator of my guilt and shortcomings. Once I've gone through everything, I'm not sure what to do with it. There are options: a bonfire, the shredder, I could leave it for the new owners, I could cook the macaroni. Whatever I do, I know I need to put it behind me. If I don't, it will sprout legs and march beside me everywhere I go.

As I pack everything away, I take deep breaths and admire each piece. "For stick figures, this painting shows tremendous sophistication. While I'm not saying you're Dostoyevsky, this letter does point to wisdom and maturity well beyond your years. Good job."

I pat myself on the back and give myself a few gold stars. I almost convince myself I am a woman of great hope and promise. But when the last homemade card for *moter's day* makes its way back into the box, I close the lid and can't tell if I'm inside or out.

Play the Dying Card

An old man sags in a recliner parked on my front lawn. He holds his arms out like a child fallen into a potty, waiting to be saved. He wears only green boxers, which he pulls high over his beach ball stomach, letting the elastic snap against his skin. As he moves, his zigzag bones poke out in strange places.

To my neighbours who scuttle by in the rain, he waves. Some stop and ask if he is okay. In response, the old man bends over and splashes his slippers in a puddle. As it gets wet, his empty duffel bag collapses. A lamp beside him flickers to lightning rhythms.

Someone taps on my backdoor. My neighbour, Edna, holds the skeleton of an umbrella over her head. "There's an old man sitting in a chair in your front yard. I think he's waiting to get inside," she whispers.

"Should I let him in?" I play with the thimbles in my pockets. Tiny bits of armour.

"He looks pretty harmless."

My neighbour has two large Himalayans that press their furry faces against her window all day. I believe she has excellent judgment. I return to my front door and open it. The man cannot raise his head so he looks at me sideways.

"Sergeant Ted, reporting for duty," he says and salutes.

I close the door on him. I, too, once thought he was harmless.

My mother and Sergeant Ted met at Wash and Tumble Laundry: Home of the Missing Sock. I liked it there since mother often let me spin in the washers instead of taking a bath. While I was jumping in and out, their underwear got mixed together. Sergeant Ted had sewn address tags into all of his clothes so mother was able to track him down and reunite him with his green boxers.

"It's the right thing to do," she said as if she was about to spoon-feed all of starving Africa. When we got there, she pulled into the driveway and told me to wait. She didn't put the underwear in a bag. She handed them over in a big bunch and a few pairs fell on the ground. I don't know why that embarrassed me but I was glad she left me in the car.

Sergeant Ted stood at the door and accepted the boxers casually, as if he was taking a basket of tomatoes from a neighbour. This was the first time I saw his daughter, Kate. Then she was just a girl, around my age, peering out from behind her father's legs. She had blonde pageant curls and wore a large Miss Alaska sash, although we lived nowhere near that state. When my mother and Sergeant Ted were finished talking, she saluted him and tiny wings sprouted from her ankle bones. I wondered what Kate might think of my mother as she stood there in her bare feet, see-through cotton dress, and angel wings.

When my mother got back in the car, she was excited she had a date with the Sergeant. "He owns a TV," she said. "And he has a daughter who I think you'll really like."

I thought she had met her prince.

On my front lawn, Edna holds the remains of her umbrella over Sergeant Ted's head while he pulls the light cord. The clouds grow darker and more faceless neighbours appear and huddle on the sidewalk. I sense their disapproval.

When I go outside, I keep my hands in my pockets, thimbles on my fingertips. My feet sink into the water and grass. Mud presses between my toes, tries to cover my feet and hold me down. Each step forward is a deliberate sloshing. It is an act. "Why did you come here?"

"There's something I want to ask you," he says.

"So ask."

"Do you remember where your mother buried her hair?"

The puddles around him form tidal waves and crash but only reach his kneecaps. Lightning threatens in the distance.

He strokes the splintered arms of his chair.

"You're not welcome here." I walk away and think of other people's family reunions—planned affairs with invitations and potato salad with too much paprika.

"Wait. I also have something to tell you," Sergeant Ted says.

"So tell."

I cried at my mom and Sergeant Ted's wedding from beginning to end. A flood so great it washed down the aisle and out the door. Everyone rowed or swam to the reception. My mother's dinghy almost tipped over. I lost my paddles.

I blamed myself for their union. At Wash and Tumble, I wanted so desperately to touch men's underwear. I had never seen it up close before and was convinced it was something terribly important I was missing out on. So when I saw it, I grabbed it and took it swimming with me. If I had just left it alone, we wouldn't have moved out of our house and I wouldn't have watched my mother wobble in high heels, stuffed into someone else's dress, her hair combed and twisted.

Sergeant Ted watches the water stream down his legs. When he bends over, he looks unhinged at the waist.

Edna says, "My cats get despondent when I'm gone for too long."

"Yes, I understand." I see the cats in the window looking despondent.

"Can we bring this man inside?" she asks.

I click my thimbles together. "He should go."

Edna looks up and down the street. "Where?" She leans in closer. "I think he's trying to tell you something. I think he's dying."

Sergeant Ted does his best to sit straight.

"Attention," he says. "Prepare to advance."

He waves my neighbours off the sidewalk. They move forward and hoist Sergeant Ted and his chair into the air.

"Charge!" Sergeant Ted says.

They take a moment to steady themselves, one neighbour positioned under each leg, and then they advance toward the house.

"I won't block your view for long," Sergeant Ted says as he glides by. He asks to be set down gently in front of the TV.

"You can't stay here."

"Thank you for letting me stay here." He settles back into his chair. "Can you please get guest soaps and towels ready? I'd like to take a bath."

My stepsister Kate was an army brat who, by age eleven, had lived in Germany, France, and Switzerland. Shortly after the underwear incident, when we were introduced, I thought she already looked tired with life. She was a chameleon, used to fitting in quickly. She could change colours in a blink: red, blue, yellow, orange, silver.

After the wedding, we moved into their army housing.

"Do you like this place?" Kate asked.

I shook my head. I had walked up to six others before I found the door that accepted my key. "They're all beige."

"Same-same. It's so everyone learns to conform," Kate said. While she waited for me to reply, she changed colours. Green, purple, pink, mauve.

"My old house was fuchsia and had magic stained-glass windows."

"What was magic about them?" Her skin paused on fuchsia.

"In the parts that were broken, you could see into another world."

"This house doesn't come with that feature but it sounds cool."

"It was. It was a different world altogether. Not this one."

"Well, if you hate this house, we won't be here long." Then she crawled under her bed and came back out with a small tray. It was packed with lipstick and other make-up. "Here," she said and handed me a tube of *Fuchsia Fix.* "Just don't let Sergeant Ted find it, or see you with it on."

"He's not the boss of me," I said.

"He's the boss of everyone." Then she told me in Switzerland, she lived in a cuckoo clock; in Germany, she lived in a beer stein; in France, she lived in a hollowed out baguette.

There were strange noises in that house. At night gurgling pipes sounded like someone being strangled; the roar of the furnace, a tiger thrown into the fire; the clicking of the fridge motor, someone tapping at the door.

I sit behind Sergeant Ted on the couch. He leaks and oozes all over my floor. He reaches for things that are not there. "Help me find my glasses," he says while he extends his hands. His fingers grapple with the air. Then he fixes imaginary frames around his ears. "These pinch my face but they're better than nothing." He settles in to watch TV, backchats the news, tells me stories about his youth that crumble and turn to dust. "We rode our horses backwards to school, sideways both ways."

"You said you came here to tell me something," I say.

"Did you hear the one about the priest and the rabbi?"

"Attention."

Sergeant Ted came into our room for an inspection. Flames licked the edges of his nostrils with each breath. Kate stood very still beside her bed while he went through her drawers. They were lined with white paper and were filled with perfectly folded clothes and balled up matching socks. He inspected her shelves—items organized by descending height. He took out his ruler and measured the space between her headboard and pillow, between her pillow and the folded blanket.

"Have you been brushing your teeth?" he yelled.

"Affirmative, Sir," Kate yelled back. He poked around in her mouth with a spanner wrench and flashlight.

Mother and I had been studying the house rules posted on the fridge but thought they were jokes written with the kind of humour we didn't understand. At our old house, we had rules on our fridge, too: *Be Nice or Leave.*

We knew there would be rules. Mother said a military life would give us structure. No-one would knock on the door asking for rent. No more floors unswept or beds unmade.

When Sergeant Ted finished with Kate, he said to me, "One free pass. Next week there will be an inspection."

When he left, Kate sat down on her bed. Pink, red, black, blue. "It's not so bad. I like to just get it over with."

The last lights in the house go off. Click, click.

I grab my binoculars and move to Sergeant Ted's side. He stares blankly at the TV. There are liver spots on his face. I connect the dots: Orion's belt, the Little Dipper, Draco. Through her window, Edna is looking at me through her binoculars. She grabs one of her cats and waves its paw. I close the blind. Sergeant Ted looks at me. "What are you doing?" he asks.

"Mapping out constellations." I look at his mouth through my binoculars. "Is there something you'd like to tell me?"

"Why did you let me in?"

"That's asking, not telling."

"Well?"

"My neighbours let you in because you played the dying card."

He clucks his tongue. "Hair still grows even after you die."

I turn the focus dial until everything blurs.

I went into the kitchen and found my mother holding her hair. It had been gathered in an elastic band and chopped off. The ends were jagged, like something had gnawed at it. She swished it around like a horse's tail. Though she still had wings, she often folded them flat against her legs and kept them tucked inside her socks.

"We could go back to our old house," I whispered. "I know how to get back in through the window." I knew it was still empty because I rode my bike by it every day.

She brushed the tail across my face. "Too late my sweet."

"He does room inspections," I told her. "Do I have to be neat?"

She nodded. A few feathers came loose and floated between us.

"I think we've made a mistake," I whispered.

"This can't be undone." Sergeant Ted had rules for her too.

"TV isn't so great," I said.

More feathers floated between us, fell to the ground, and then she swept them up.

The hallway floorboards have something to say.

Sergeant Ted shakes as he gets out of his chair. The leather sticks to his legs and fights to hang on to his pale, loose skin. "I'd like to change into my uniform, please."

"So change."

When he shuffles out of the bathroom, he is wearing a billowy faded uniform, a leather pudding-bowl helmet, and goggles. He sits down, lights his pipe. Then he spreads his arms and legs and straddles an imaginary motorcycle. "Vroom," he says and twists the throttle.

"You came here to tell me something," I remind him.

"Did I ever tell you about the time I spent in Germany?" He closes his eyes. "I hit a landmine and flew ass over teakettle into the ditch. They couldn't find me for two days."

"Those must have been two very good days."

He revs the engine again and smokes his pipe. "When they finally found me, my laces were still tied up. My boots were still on my feet but my soles were missing."

I listen to his raspy laughter, to the gurgle of old tar in his oesophagus. He closes his eyes again and finds the same bombs exploding beneath him, stealing bits of memory and his soles.

My mother said she was going out to bury her hair. It was bad luck to just throw it away. "We don't need any more bad luck, do we?"

"No," I said. Sergeant Ted was bad enough.

"Do you need anything from the store?" she asked.

"I guess I'll need matching socks and a new toothbrush."

"Bring me your old one so I'll know what kind to get."

I went to get my toothbrush, a frayed thing with a worn out Mickey Mouse on the handle. When I came back, she was already gone.

Shadows slip underneath the door.

Sergeant Ted is tired after his motorcycle ride around Germany. He settles back down in his chair. "I've only lost my two front teeth. The rest are mine," he tells me and gives a big smile.

I grab one of my dress forms and start to sew on a zipper. I'm making a spacesuit for one of my clients. I can't be distracted by Sergeant Ted's tartar-free gums, his crooked but otherwise healthy incisors. I've got work to do. Deadlines to meet. My client is heading to the moon any day now.

Sergeant Ted sleeps, mouth gaping open. I grab my flashlight, move closer and take a look inside. I see letters hiding behind rotten molars, tucked underneath silver fillings, buried by the weight of his tongue. I take my tweezers and extract the letters one by one. I hold them in my palm and try to arrange them. These are foreign words, if they are words at all.

Sergeant Ted wakes with a snort. "You're sitting very close," he says.

115

"I wanted to see you."

He covers his eyes with both hands then takes them away and says, "Peek-a-boo, I see you too."

I wash my hands and watch a, b, and c swirl down the drain.

When it rained feathers, I knew my mother died on the way to bury her hair. Sergeant Ted picked up a few feathers and said, "Who kills chickens in the city?"

When I told him what happened, he looked at Kate and me and said, "What am I supposed to feed you two?"

At her funeral, my mother sat beside me. "Shouldn't you be up there?" I moved my head in the direction of the coffin. "Not just yet."

"This might be fun." I thought of all the ways my invisible mother could help me. When the service was over, I got up to leave but I didn't know she wasn't behind me. Sergeant Ted's fingers were a handcuff around my wrist. He pulled me out into the cold. I stared at the open car door then the long sidewalk. I looked at Kate, already inside, turning blue. "There are fewer shadows when you're around," she said.

She held out her shaking hand, icicles forming on her fingertips. I reached out and tried to warm them.

Hand on the doorknob. Turn, then release. Turn, then release.

"Invite these people to my funeral," Sergeant Ted says. He shakes a small address book at me. When I look inside, most of the names, written in pencil, have been erased. The book is filled with the edges of torn out pages, smudges where names used to be.

Kate and I made a confession booth out of a cardboard refrigerator box and an old shower curtain. We used edible candy necklaces for rosaries. We turned off the lights because we thought it would be easier to confess.

"Bless me father for I have sinned," Kate said.

"How long since your last confession, my child?"

"I've never confessed. I have quite a list." I could hear her munching her rosary.

"Where would you like to start?"

"My mother died giving birth to me."

"Why is that something you want to confess?"

"I feel guilty."

"It was not your fault. Child, you are forgiven. Which part of the rosary is your favourite?"

"Watermelon. I'm going to save the rest of my list for later," she said and pulled the shower curtain aside. We switched places.

"Bless me father for I have sinned."

"What did you do?"

"I touched your father's underwear."

"Me, too," she said. "That's also on my list." I parted the shower curtain to see her stroke it off her paper. Her skin turned blue and stayed that way for a long time.

Wait. Wait. Wait.

Sergeant Ted's chair creaks as he leans over to strike a match on its wood frame. He is dying of lung cancer but at 75 insists, "It's been bloody long enough."

"I agree."

He taps his pipe. He starts every one with three puffs then smokes until my living-room is filled with a fog neither of us can find our way through. "Do you know where Kate is?" he asks.

"No, do you want me to try and find her?" I've heard being surrounded by family can help a person die faster.

He nods, then falls asleep. His pipe spills. I watch a large ash smoulder on the chair then burn itself out.

To solve the meal problem, Sergeant Ted gave Kate and me

army ration packs for our school lunches. "Just add water," he said.

We sold the dehydrated flakes to boys who found the gelatinous substance very useful. We used the money to buy food and make-up. In our beige world, a blossoming collection seemed very important. We bought lipstick in shades of *Sassy Spice*, *Wow Violet*, and *Surge Butter*. We bought blush in shades of *Smouldering Wine* and *Iced Lotus*.

In the morning, after Sergeant Ted left for work, we would apply liberally and repeat as necessary. I narrowed her wide nose. She widened my narrow-set eyes. We contoured each other's inadequate cheekbones. We did everything we could to blend, blend, blend. At school, we spent six hours thoroughly and blissfully trolloped. Then we would race home and slip back into our blotchy, oily skin.

The dark cloud passes over my bed.

Though years pass between our conversations, Kate picks up exactly where we left off.

"I told the drycleaner my suit is now two different colours. But he never did give me a refund. Anyway, how are you?"

She is one of those people who like to seem busier than they really are so little effort is required on my part. "Sergeant Ted is dying. He'd like to see you."

"It's good to want things," she says.

Throughout our conversation, she punctuates pauses so it will seem like her words must first sail across an ocean to reach me.

"I'm not coming," she says. She is also the type of person who thinks her decisions mean more when they hurt people.

"You're coming for me, not him," I say.

When I get off the phone, I poke Sergeant Ted awake. I love the startled grunt he makes. The way his feet find their place on the ground. The way he looks around for snipers then sees a *Price is Right* rerun, Bob Barker on TV reminding him to spay or neuter his pet.

"Kate is on her way."

"I'll stay alive until she gets here," he says.

"While we're waiting, is there something you'd like to tell me?" I watch the three white hairs on the top of his head wave back and forth.

"I don't suppose you remember...."

"Go on."

"Where our dog Abe was buried?"

I pluck the three hairs from his head and surrender too easily, because it's all I can do.

The boys at school started wanting more than Kate's rations. One made the mistake of showing up at our house. He asked Sergeant Ted, casually, if she was allowed to hang out with him.

"Not tonight," said Sergeant Ted, and we waited for the door to slam, for the earth to shake, for him to come into our room and breathe fire. Instead, he went back to the kitchen and we heard him rummaging through the fridge.

Before we went to bed, he said, "I don't want you two walking home by yourselves tomorrow. There's a pervert on the loose."

After our last class, we wiped off our make-up in the school bathroom. We walked outside and saw an army tank parked on the lawn. Sergeant Ted popped the lid and gave a parade wave to the gathering crowd. The boy from the night before crawled out charred and shredded. Kate walked forward, turned a brilliant shade of *Just Pinched*, then sank into the pit. I stood paralyzed as Sergeant Ted climbed out, lifted me up and carried me on my side like a plank. Kate's relationship with boys returned strictly to the selling of dehydrated flakes.

In my old house, you could look through broken stained glass and go anywhere.

Headlights flash across the living-room window. I hear Kate cut the engine. I look through the blinds and see her sitting in a rented convertible, staring straight ahead, hands still locked on the wheel. It is raining. The car is filled with water. A little girl sits beside her wearing a lifejacket and snorkel. There is a light breeze blowing Kate's scarf. She looks like she's still driving. The static from my TV is her soundtrack. From the streetlight glow, her skin looks radiant, cheekbones contoured. Her hair is gathered in a loose knot. I put on my thimbles and wait.

I heard the window slide open in the middle of the night. Felt the smack of cold air. Was someone coming or going? I shook my firefly jar and found Kate's bed empty. There was a silver fingerprint on the glass. In *Crushed Orange* lipstick, she wrote *MIA* over her bed.

I heard Sergeant Ted turn off the last lights. Click. Click. He opened our bedroom door and saw Kate was gone. "Where is she?"

"I don't know." I used my firefly jar to keep him away.

"You bloody freak." He ripped Kate's drawers out. Balls of socks went flying. Books, tallest to shortest, crashed off the shelves.

He tore the mattress off the bed. I feared *Forever Fuchsia,* and *Breathless Berry* would spill across the floor, but they stayed hidden in our secret tray. He went back to the drawers and found a container of *Cherry Blossom* lip gloss hidden in a pair of Kate's underwear. He sniffed it. For a moment the wrinkles ironed themselves off his face. Then he was on top of me, digging into cherry and smearing it across my face.

The bedsprings moan under the weight of him.

When Kate releases the wheel, I close my eyes and listen to the sound of rushing water, then the clip-clop of high heels on pavement. Kate doesn't knock. She walks through the door, clicks her briefcase on the floor and slides out of her shoes as if she's just returning home from work.

"Hi," I say and hand them towels. The little girl looks at me from behind Kate's legs. Big Kate and Little Kate.

"Hi," Big Kate says. She tries to detach Little Kate from her legs.

"Hello." I wave to Little Kate.

"Hello," she says. "In London, we live inside Big Ben and I go to school on The Tube."

"That sounds like fun." Pointing to Big Kate's ridiculous crocodile bag, I say, "I like that."

"Cranberry red. Wasn't that your favourite?"

"Fuchsia."

"Ah, yes. I remember." She looks around. "It's creepy in here with all of the mannequins."

"They're dress forms. Only a few are mannequins."

Kate looks at her father. "Did I make it?"

"Did I make it?" Little Kate imitates while talking through her snorkel.

"She does that when she's nervous," Big Kate says, swatting at the girl.

"She does that when she's nervous," Little Kate repeats. She starts doing the breaststroke around my living-room.

I climbed out the window and followed her silver footprints until they disappeared. When they stopped, I stopped. I stood there and knew she would never leave me. Without her, he only had me.

I waited years for her return.

"Well?" Kate says, waving her phone. "Did I make it?"

"Well? Did I make it?" Little Kate says.

Big Kate puts her hand over Little Kate's mouth. Little Kate tries to bite her mother's fingers. Big Kate lets go.

"You can't control them," Big Kate says. She walks over to Sergeant Ted. She grabs the remote from his hand and turns off the TV. She reaches out to touch his head but hovers over it instead. Then she pulls away, as if she's been stung.

Little Kate walks over and stares. Sergeant Ted's pipe dangles from his mouth like an upside down comma—a sentence left unfinished. A string of saliva pulls from his lips as Big Kate takes the pipe and lights it for herself. "Thank god I was on business in New York and not London or it would have taken me forever to get here."

"Yes, that was convenient," I say.

Sergeant Ted startles awake. Little Kate stands in front of him. "Are you going to die while I'm standing right here watching?"

"I hope not," Sergeant Ted says.

Big Kate blows smoke in his face. He coughs and turns toward her. "Hello, Katie. Thank you for coming. You turned out just fine."

She hands back his pipe. "Keep smoking."

"Keep smoking!" Little Kate says.

"Did I ever tell you about the time I spent in Germany?" he asks Little Kate.

"Nope." Little Kate pulls up a chair.

Sergeant Ted is tired but manages to spin tales in which he is always the hero, in which he stands in harm's way to protect others. He saves little girls from burning castles. He helps lost people find their way home. There are explosions, which, he admits, have altered his memory somewhat. He keeps talking, and talking. His breathing gets shallower and more forced.

Big Kate takes his pipe and smokes until a cloud forms over his head. Finally, just outside Düsseldorf, a bomb takes him out.

"This old guy's sleepy," Little Kate says.

Big Kate turns a colour that can only be described as joy.

When the paramedics arrive, Big Kate says, "Do not resuscitate."

They pack him up and the chair sits empty. Sergeant Ted

once told me it had an eject mechanism, and if I dared to sit in it, it would send me to the moon. I pull on my client's spacesuit and get Little Kate to zip it up. I slowly lower myself into the chair. I feel the frame and springs press into my bones, dig into my skin. The leather is worn and feels like years of shedding skin. I close my eyes, grip the armrests, and have never felt farther from the moon.

Little Kate looks around at the dress forms. "Are you my aunt?" she asks.

"Are you my aunt?" I ask her back.

"No." She starts laughing.

I see the appeal of her game but Big Kate turns *Volcanic Red*. "I guess I'm your aunt. Sort of."

"Auntie Sort-Of, can you make me a ball gown? Apparently, I'm going to a funeral."

"Sergeant Ted wishes to be buried sitting in his chair," the lawyer reads.

The funeral director doesn't think a chair coffin is a good idea. Then he works out the price and says, "I'd be happy to accommodate your father's most unusual final request."

"Stepfather," I correct as he hands me the estimate.

"He must have been quite a character," he says.

"Yes, quite a character," Big Kate says.

"Yes, quite a character," Little Kate says.

"Don't take your death lying down," Big Kate says as we're leaving. She looks at me and says, "That's British humour." "That's why it's not funny," Little Kate tells me.

The red taffeta for Little Kate's dress comes down the chimney, slips underneath the door, pours out the taps, fills up my tub, overflows my kitchen sink. Little Kate stands on a chair, eyes closed, arms held out at her sides. She doesn't wiggle when the cold tape measure goes around her.

"Is there enough fabric for a train, Auntie Sort-Of?"

"I think so."

Big Kate floats on a life raft in the red sea and tells us how dresses are made in Italy. She stresses the importance of boning, says it gives structure but can make it difficult to breathe. She paddles over to dry land and offers to help. She grabs the material underneath Little Kate's armpit and gouges her while pinning the fabric together. Little Kate grabs my pinking shears and makes crinkled threats.

"Testy, testy," Big Kate says. She puts the pins down and holds her hands in the air. Then she grabs a mannequin and starts to dance. I help Little Kate down and find her a small partner. I grab my own mannequin. We are all on dry land dancing fearlessly with our neutered men.

Little Kate, in her red ball gown, walks up to Sergeant Ted— hands on her hips. Big Kate and I sit in the first row and stare at his open coffin. It looks like an outhouse made of lacquered mahogany. He sits upright in his chair, hands folded on his lap.

"The funeral director said he'll have to be buried deeper than six feet," I tell Big Kate.

"How deep?"

"At least twelve feet."

"That's a good depth."

When Little Kate is finished inspecting Sergeant Ted, she stands back and twirls around and around. She holds her dress up, showing flashes of white underwear.

Big Kate gets up. I grab her icy blue hand and we walk toward him. I poke Sergeant Ted's face. His skin is firm but supple. The dent I made doesn't fill in so I make a few more. He is a wax doll wearing make-up. *Tiptoe Through the Tulips* on his cheeks, *Tomato Yum* on his lips.

Big Kate pinches the sides of his mouth, revealing the wires that are keeping it shut.

"I'm sorry," he says, with deep remorse.

"You came all this way to tell me that?" I say. "You shouldn't have."

124

Formaldehyde dribbles down his chin. I unfold his rubbery hands and jam my thimbles onto his fingertips. Then I grab one of Little Kate's hands and Big Kate grabs the other. Together, we stop the little girl from spinning.

ELIZA ROBERTSON was born in Vancouver, and completed her undergraduate degree at the University of Victoria. She moved to England to take a Masters in Prose Fiction at the University of East Anglia, where she won the Man Booker Scholarship, and now lives in Toulouse, where she is working on a novel. Her stories have appeared in journals in Canada, the United Kingdom and the United States, and have been shortlisted for National Magazine Awards and the McClelland & Stewart Journey Prize.

KEVIN COUTURE was born and raised in British Columbia and has worked at the largest open-pit mine in North America, a not-so-large lakeside resort, a greasy spoon and a periodontal office. His work has appeared in *Grain, The Fiddlehead, The Antigonish Review, The Dalhousie Review, Event, Prairie Fire,* and *PRISM international.* He is currently finishing a collection of stories about, but not really about, animals.

JILL SEXSMITH grew up in Manitoba and has lived and worked in Australia and Japan. She has a BA from the University of Winnipeg and an MFA in Creative Writing from UBC, and is a recipient of the Carol Shields Creative Writing Award. Her stories have appeared in such literary journals as *The Walrus, PRISM international, The Fiddlehead* and *The New Quarterly.* She lives in Winnipeg, where she works in communications for the University of Manitoba.

MARK ANTHONY JARMAN has published four collections of stories, *Dancing Nightly in the Tavern, New Orleans Is Sinking, 19 Knives* and *My White Planet,* a collection of poetry, *Killing the Swan,* and a travel book, *Ireland's Eye.* His hockey novel *Salvage King Ya!* is on Amazon.ca's list of 50 Essential Canadian Books, and he has won the Gold Medal at the National Magazine Awards. He is the fiction editor of *Fiddlehead* and teaches at UNB.

Previous volumes in this series featured the following writers:

Most of these books are still available. Please inquire.